I0714560

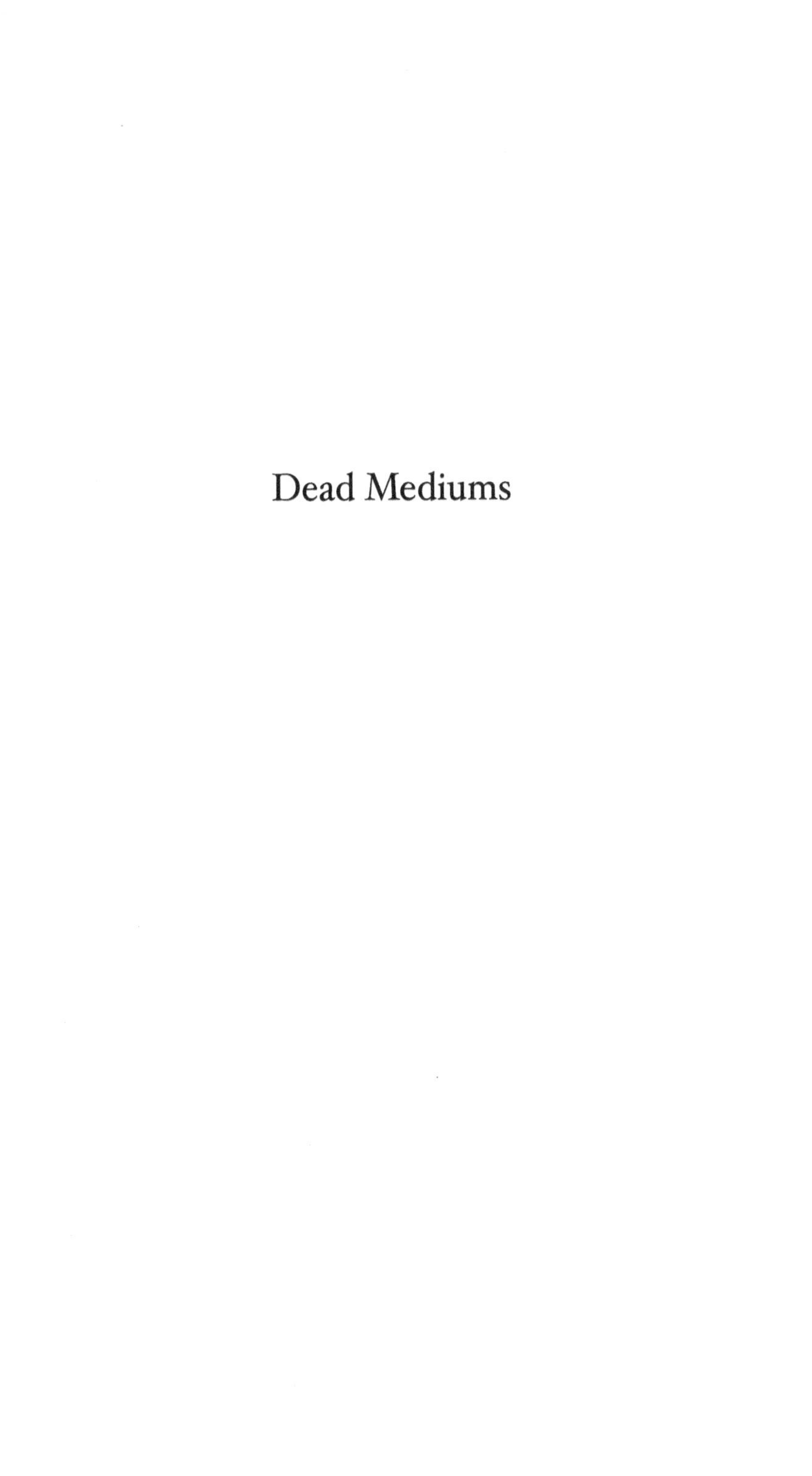

# Dead Mediums

# PRAISE FOR *DEAD MEDIUMS*

"Dan Leach's stories swoop and veer from hilarious to bizarre to poignant and sometimes coalesce into all three within a single paragraph. His voice is unique, so tighten your seat belts, because *Dead Mediums* will take you on a wild, wild ride."

**Ron Rash, author of *Serena* and *Burning Bright***

"In *Dead Mediums*, Dan Leach writes with masterful velocity without sacrificing heart."

**T. Geronimo Johnson, author of *Welcome to Braggsville* and *Hold It 'Til It Hurts***

"Late in Dan Leach's fantastic new book, a character says, 'I am a Southerner and therefore ruined by ambiguity.' This is the rich territory Leach explores in *Dead Mediums*—the gray, unmapped, ambiguous terrain of relationships, and his exploration has yielded a truly phenomenal collection, one that should establish Leach's reputation as a contemporary master of the Southern short story. If it doesn't, there is no justice in the literary world. This collection absolutely gleams with artistry and passion. The voices that tell these tales run a crazy, wonderful gamut, from the quiet magical realism of 'Fixers' to the gritty, Larry Brown-esque realism of 'The Devil Is Beating His Wife.' These characters—and the stories they tell—live with you long after you turn the final page. You can't ask for more than that."

**Scott Gould, author of *The Hammerhead Chronicles and* and *Things That Crash, Things That Fly***

"Dan Leach brings American myth to South Carolina with a cast of dreamers, dark-horses, family men, and sexed-up maniacs. *Dead Mediums* makes clean fantasy of everyday, imperfect life. While ordinary people encounter wizards and commune with the dead, Leach's clear-eyed prose keeps readers close to the tensions between people in concert. This is an honest, playful, soulful book."

**Stephen Hundley, author of**
***The Aliens Will Come to Georgia First***

"Dan Leach is the South's answer to Haruki Murakami. The confrontational stories in this collection are like magic spells drunk on moonshine, weaving their woozy divinations into your head. Because they are meant to describe you, me, and our modern age, they can't help but be as conniving as a Rick Flair promo, as mean as a two-dollar firecracker, and as Christ-haunted as Flannery O'Connor's subconscious. You will keep thinking about these knowing, sunburnt fables long after you've finished this book"

**Matthew Thomas Meade, author of *Rocketflower***

"One of my favorite things in this world is reading a good story, told well. When I read Dan's stories that's exactly what I got. *Dead Mediums* is well worth your time and money."

**Justin Peter Kinkel-Schuster,**
**singer-songwriter behind Constant Stranger**
**and Take Care, Take Care**

# DEAD MEDIUMS

## Stories

*by Dan Leach*

Trident Press
Boulder, CO

ISBN: 978-1-951226-17-6

Cover by Rachel Pfeffer

Published by Trident Press
940 Pearl St.
Boulder, CO 80302

tridentcafe.com/trident-press-titles

Grateful acknowledgment is made to the publications in which these stories first appeared: "Wasp Queen" in *Copper Nickel*; "The Five Stages of Hunger" in *Yalobusha Review*; "Brother Bill Leaves the Narrow Path" in *Smokelong Quarterly*; "Places Without Porches" in *The New Madrid Review*; "The Devil Is Beating His Wife" in *The Potomac Review*; "Whale Fall" in *Bayou Magazine*.

# CONTENTS

# WASP QUEEN

---

I.

Convention says I should kill you. By convention I mean my wife, the artist, who had plans to repurpose the vintage steel trash can inside of which you've built a nest the size of a small child. By convention I also mean my four-year old daughter, who has been afraid to play outside since the day she bumped the trash can, prompting your drones to emerge and sting her on her face, and across her stomach, and even in the tiny pockets of flesh behind her knees. Twenty-six hits? Some might call that excessive.

II.

When I invite people to think about you, everyone's an expert. *Burn them*, says my dad. *Wait until night, when they are sleeping, then douse the nest in gasoline and chuck a match inside.* My brother submits a different method: *Let's duct-tape the lid on. We'll dump it in the country and make it someone else's problem.* An old man at the hardware store tries to sell me something he calls a bug bomb. The old man says, *The best thing about the bomb is that it kills the bitch.* I say, *The bitch?* He apologizes. *The queen*, he says. *It's guaranteed to kill the queen.*

III.

Everyone who hears about you requests a picture, and every-one who receives a picture feels two sequential feelings. First, they are impressed by the size of your colony. Second, they are excited about the possibilities for destruction. My friend from Chicago sends me an article that reveals how each spring you lay approximately fifty-thousand eggs then train up legions of soldier-children to protect the nest. My friend from Seattle tells me, *Whatever you decide on, film it. That kind of shit goes viral.* I thank all my friends for their enthusiastic support in imagining all the ways you might die.

IV.

I share the viable tactics with my wife. She hates any plan that would damage the trash can. The artistic project she en-visions requires a clean, history-free object. No burn marks, no stains. On this she is clear—there must be no you, but also no sign of me removing you. With help from a young man at the hardware store, she secures a poisonous spray that prom-ises to achieve this end. *It's simple*, says my wife. *Spray this at night and in the morning they'll be dead.* I ask, *The queen too?* My wife nods. *The queen too.* When I mention the article that asks if creatures such as bees and crabs could be said to have sen-tience, my wife falls silent for a moment then says, *How would you feel about lasagna tonight?*

V.

Which brings us here, to this moonless spring night, where I stand in our backyard wearing three layers of clothing and gripping two cans of poisonous spray. Here where I stare down into the trash can and try to see you, or your family, or at least some part of what you've built. What I see, though, is nothing. So dark is the night that the trash can resembles the black throat of a bottomless well. I have to aim the poison not at you but at where I believe you are. I have to imagine you there. I aim but don't yet squeeze the nozzle. I hesitate. Listen—there is so much I want to tell you.

# PLACES WITHOUT PORCHES

When the cancer in her dad's blood got bad Sophia and I went up to Nebraska. We knocked snow off our boots and watched the old man writhe. We held mugs of hot liquid and watched the body sputter then stop. Day of the funeral Sophia asked if we could stick around.

"They need me," she whispered, wet face pressed into my shoulder.

Her mom and sister were in the kitchen, eating nothing and filling the rooms with laughter-turned-weeping-turned-silence-etc. From our place on the couch we heard a fork get flung against the wall. Sophia's body trembled. She repeated the proposition: "One year is all I'm asking."

Nebraska: land of snow, corn, and legions of smug white folks cold and large as castles. Some futures require both love and death for your consideration.

I kissed Sophia on her forehead. We quit our jobs in South Carolina and said we'd give it a year.

For twelve months after Sophia's father died, family became our nine-to-five. Meals were cooked and delivered, home-videos watched and wept over. "What do you want to do tonight?" was no longer a thing. When her mom got sad, we were there. When her sister threatened some senseless act of self-harm, we were there. For one whole year, when the flames of grief flared, we showed up with buckets in hand. "It's just a year," my logic ran.

Dim the lights and cue the cellos; ours was a love for the big screen.

Eventually there came a conversation about the future.

"I want to go," was my basic position, and I gave good, logical reasons in support of it.

"I want to stay," was her basic position, and she gave good, logical reasons in support of it.

"But you said one year," I argued. "That was the agreement."

"That wasn't an agreement," she replied. "It was a prediction."

After an hour of dead ends and repetitions, game was called on account of rain. Sophia to the bedroom to phone her mom. Me to the couch with a mug of mostly bourbon. Behold the veneer of compromise peeled back like the skin of a grape.

Back in Carolina, Dabo was kicking Alabama's ass all over national television and every other week some childhood friend called me up to report on the incalculable joy of life in the South. Oh the mountains! Oh the beaches! Oh the green sprawling cities that make the streets of where you are seem lovely as used floss!

I didn't mind their gloating. They were only reminding me of what I already knew. Carolina is the song you hum to see you through the tragedy of Nebraska.

"I thought you said it was just for a year," said my own mother, after I told her that, regarding a return date, we were "playing it by ear."

"I did."

"So come home already."

"I can't."

"Why not?"

"I love her."

"Does she love you?"

"It's not about that."

"Okay," said my mother. "What is it about, then?"

"Sacrifice," I said and almost believed it. "It's about sacrifice."

"Sacrifice, huh?" said my mother and laughed like a joke had been made. "My son, the living sacrifice."

Different night, different fight, I said, "What about my family? Don't they count for something?"

"Everyone you love is still alive," she said.

That was the end of that one.

Try this: no one in Nebraska has a front porch. Regarding this mysterious omission, I'll submit three theories.

Theory number one: since the temperature in Nebraska only gets above ten degrees for about two weeks in July, the builders have concluded it's too cold for porches.

Theory number two: since everyone in Nebraska grew up on farms and consider idle time an unpardonable sin, the builders have concluded it's too busy for porches.

Theory number three: since Midwesterners tend to limit their powers of speech to short bursts on football or the weather, the builders have concluded it's too quiet for porches.

Because I shit you not—there are no front porches in Nebraska. Just ceaseless wind that leaves bruises on your cheeks and a bunch of windows gone blue with the light of bad television. Just snow and no stories.

I told Sophia it was time to go home. Told her I'd weep with her like Jesus over her dad's untimely death, but it was time for us to go back to Carolina.

When she asked me why I hated Nebraska so much, I said, "Too cold, too busy, too quiet." Told her the lack of porches was emblematic and that no one with a heart that hurts for life could be happy in a place intent on wooing its own ugliness.

Her family had thoughts on the matter. All I had to do was leave the room and—poof!—instant dialogue.

"He wants to rip you away from your family because he doesn't like being cold?" said her sister. "We're grieving. Plus, this is your home. Tell him to grow some balls and think about someone other than himself."

This from a woman who in two years never once combined her words to form anything other than "How's work?" or "You doing okay?" This from a brat who'd never crossed state lines.

Her mother? Even worse. "Just because he goes doesn't mean you have to follow. It's not like you two are married."

Try returning to a room filled with the colorless, odorless ether of fake love. It stings the eyes and pumps the heart with acid. Had there been a porch, I might've stepped outside.

Confession: for a minute there, the drinking got out of hand. In the evenings I'd sip myself into a fog and watch vitriol slip out of my mouth like fat men from a water slide. In the mornings the bourbon to black coffee ratio was just plain absurd.

"Why?" Sophia asked, about every other day.

I couldn't answer.

They asked Faulkner the same thing. "For the pain," was his response.

Damn right, old son. For all that ice-cold Midwestern pain.

Out of the blue my old boss in Carolina called me up.

"Wanted to put something on your radar," he said and told me about an opening.

"Appreciate you thinking of me," I said and told him I'd talk it over with Sophia.

When I did, I played all my cards at once.

I said, "The salary's almost twice what I make here. And my mom just told me about a two-bed-two-bath a half mile out of downtown. And I think your family's doing okay now. And Sam said everyone at church misses us. And, oh, there's a new place called The Swamp Rabbit Cafe with a little grocery that's all-local and all-organic and has a bike trail that goes straight to Travelers Rest. And it's seventy degrees in Greenville right now. And we could get bikes, baby. Think about that. We could be homeowners and bike-riders. Wouldn't that be nice?"

Her response?

"You do what you need to do."

She went into the bedroom and, after the crying, called her mother.

From the window, drink in hand, I watched snow fall. It slid indifferently through the air, filling the beds of all those pickup trucks like a row of little white graves. I watched the sad glow of all those blue windows. "Carolina. Carolina. Care. Oh. Line. Uh." It doesn't matter how well you know the words. Sometimes you need the sound.

What mystery is this? That two people who barely like each other can climb into bed, bring skin to bitter skin, and make it. Did it not matter that she was sad, and that I was hateful, and that each of us by then resented the other? Miraculously, it didn't. Sophia gave it up. Even when I was drunk, Sophia gave it up. Even on weeks we barely spoke, there we were, every other night, our love like a phantom limb still tingling in its pretense long after the real thing's gone. Sex and misery alive on the same mattress: I don't know a greater mystery.

Could a little language have saved us? It's possible. Back home a trip to Piggly Wiggly on Tuesday night converts into an epic poem before the sacks hit the floor. In Nebraska you flat out ask someone what they're all about or where the hell they came from and you get—what?—a bumper sticker? A dull sputtering of short facts like possession of a personality is a class-A felony?

Maybe I could've felt more for her family if they bothered to answer my questions with something other than "Good" and "Okay" and "Mmhmm."

Maybe I wouldn't have constantly dreamt about leaving if everyone wasn't so damn ugly in their silence. Midwestern men in their big trucks looked constantly like they were fantasizing your murder. Their women looked like them, in wigs. No one lingered in the hallways at work and even the liquor store clerks denied you anything more than the basic motions of decency.

And there was my Sophia, quiet as the rest. "I don't know," the new answer to "What can I do to help?" and "Why won't you talk to me?" and "How long are you going to go on like this?" Sophia, my girl, tongue-tied in her grief and looking each day a little less like the firecracker I fell for while walking all those green-gold paths at Clemson and talking about the future.

How far down would she ride the when-in-Rome train? Would she get a bad haircut and start drinking Busch Light? Would I find her planted in front of Fox News, cursing the government and maligning the "liberals" out in Colorado? Would she forget it was she who once said she'd volunteer for a frontal lobotomy before returning to Nebraska?

I didn't know, and she wasn't saying.

Such is the way with silence—it leads to hellish speculation and spells of paranoia. Led a bum like me into the awful land of rage and self-pity.

"Do you even want me to stay?" I asked her.

"I don't know. I'm sorry, but I just don't know."

In that ice-encrusted vacuum where the right words elude you and even the wrong ones show up late, I let myself get hateful. No stories to take you somewhere else. No fortuitous accidents of phrasing to lift you up or give language to the pain. It's not something I'm proud of: my heart became a booming factory town of ugliness.

And yet, surely some ownership is called for. So what if Nebraska was Siberia with supermarkets? A cup can't spill what it doesn't contain. Something inside of me stunk like death, and geography can only take so much blame. No, I hated things and people and weather because—why else?—I'm hateful. I watched the woman I love stumble around in grief over her dead father, watched her fail to reach her broken family, and I was hateful, hateful, hateful.

She called me Lazarus when I said I was leaving.
"I know these two years have been hard on you," she said. "It'll be good for you to get back to the land of the living."
"Think you'll ever come back down South?" I asked her.
Then came the chorus of our time in Nebraska.
"I don't know," she said. "I just don't know."
In her defense, who the hell does?

Reactions to my departure were varied.
My boss: "I respect the hell out of you for giving up those two years to be close to her family. You're a good man."
Her sister: "Can't say I'm surprised. He must be the most juvenile and selfish person I've ever met."
My mother: "You know I love Sophia. I really do. But you deserve someone who's willing to consider *your* dreams and *your* needs. This is for the best. She'll be happier up there."
Her grandmother: "What a bastard."
My best friend: "What a bitch."
Her mother: "It's not like you two are married."
My father: "At least you two aren't married."

Her: "I hope you know I still love you."

Me: "I hope you know the same."

The whole Sophia thing taught me this: clay has nothing on truth. A little pressure and the world becomes whatever you need it to be.

I'm on the road now, called forth and holding my car on a steady line towards Carolina. It's a two day drive, and, radio busted, I have no choice but to roll my window down and keep company with Sophia's various highway ghosts. There's one who talks my ear off straight through Kansas City, calling me a coward and saying things like "Enjoy the beach, asshole." There's another who keeps quiet and, when engaged, leans against the window and whispers "What's the point?" I've talked to half a dozen by the time I reach St. Louis, but still not the one who lets me see the old smile and says, "It's over, now. Move forward." Still not the one who hears about the porches and, sliding her hand out into the rushing black air of the night, fills the cab with the sound of her laughter.

# BROTHER BILL LEAVES
# THE NARROW PATH

---

In the church you grew up in, men who hated liberals and queers spoke in God's voice. They taught you about the world, burning holiness into your bones and stuffing your dreams with sulfur. You imagined your school friends on fire and added that feeling to what eternity might be like. These men screamed down truth in King James English and asked for your Amen. You gave it to them. You were a kid.

Then came time for college. The Sunday before you left, you knelt beside their pulpit, and they covered you with hands and heavy breathing, asking God to go before you. Your aunt called you Jonah and said to show the pagans at Clemson how true believers live. They gave you a black leather Bible with your name imprinted on the front. They told you about the narrow path and how not to leave it.

You could not have known that Clemson, just a hundred miles up Interstate 26, would be a different planet. The people there heard you speak and asked where you were from. When you told them, they shook their heads and said they had never heard of it. You could think of a few things that they had never heard of. Tongues. Blood moons. Snake handling. The faces at Clemson, especially the eyes, taught you to keep quiet. College taught you to forget.

It wasn't easy. The first time you got drunk you fell face-down in a field and begged Him not to smite you. You woke up the next morning with throbbing in your head and dirt caked on your knuckles. Your roommate, a business major from Greenville, said he saw you throwing rocks at the sky and screaming out "Jehovah Jireh!" You laughed and blamed the beer. There are things a business major from Greenville will never understand. Forgetting, for one.

At Christmas, when you went to back, the church was just as you left it. After the hymns but before the sermon, the pastor called you out by name. He asked you to stand up and share how God was using you to advance the kingdom. Because there you were, standing in front of all those old familiar faces, and because you had to say something, you lied and talked about sharing your faith with your roommate, the unbeliever. They called you a light on a hill and asked for prayer requests. "Temptation" was all you said. They laid their hands on you and asked Jesus to keep you on the narrow path.

You went back to Clemson after New Year's. You swore this time you'd write.

You met a girl on Easter weekend, when the campus was cleared out for the holiday and the bars were running specials. And after you went back to her dorm and did what you did on the bed in her dormitory with its cheap sheets and squeaky springs, you didn't throw any rocks at the sky. In fact, after it was over, you felt about the same. A couple months later you saw this girl on the bridge in front of the library. Had you known her name, you might've called it.

What they say about never shitting a shitter is false. You learned this during those summer you went home. The people there asked questions and you answered them. No one suspected a thing. They just smiled, like children in their faith.

Junior year a boy from your church got accepted into

the agricultural program. You would see him in the student union, handing out tracts and asking people about where they thought they would go when they died. Most days you got your food and slipped by unnoticed. But the times he saw you first, he would embrace you with a hug and call you Brother Bill. Then you would apologize and say that you'd been busy. He said something about lunch. You called him Brother Isaac and agreed to coffee sometime soon.

Later that semester, to prove a point, a English professor ripped a page out of the Bible and ground it beneath his heel. Several students applauded. One got up and left. You sat there and wondered what it was you were supposed to feel.

Your own Bible, the one with the black leather and name engraved, was gone. It started on your nightstand before getting moved to your shelf. At one point, it was at the bottom of a box of magazines in your bathroom. Somewhere along the way it wandered off to somewhere other than your dorm.

What never left was the music. Nights your roommates left you would take your guitar out on the porch and, without trying, your fingers would find the chords. *Come thou fount of every blessing*, you would hum but never sing. *Tune my heart to sing thy praise*, you would think but never hum.

After graduation you took a job in Nebraska. You bought a house in a quiet little town where no one asked questions. You met a quiet little woman and, after a couple years together, asked her to be your wife. This, now, is your life. To work a job you neither love nor hate. To go home to the one who loves you. To watch TV and fall asleep.

But you know it's coming: the day when someone asks. Because even in Nebraska people ask about God. What you say is up to you. Maybe you'll tell them where you're from. Or maybe you'll tell them where you're going.

# FIXERS

The postcards from Juna still show up at my place, but if there is a pattern, I have failed to discern it. Sometimes she sends me a card per week. Sometimes months pass with no word. I am holding her latest one now. It's Christmas morning, and I am searching for a clue.

Her card is dated December 22nd. On the side meant for text, there is nothing. On the other side: Juna. She is bundled in winter clothing and standing on a balcony that is backlit by the whiteness of snow-covered mountains. A ski resort in Yuzawa, I believe. Possibly Hakuba. She does not appear to have changed much from the last postcard, which arrived from Tangier in early November. Her black hair is still short, her large, toothy smile is still devastating in its confidence, and (of course) she is still blind in her left eye.

There is one subtle difference here. In this one, she is not facing her photographer, as has been her habit in the other postcards. Instead, she has adjusted her shoulders and tilted her head, so as to hide the right side of her face and present to the camera just one eye—the blind one. She is leaning forward as if to throw the eye's grey essence first at her photographer and now, so many miles and days later, at me. It is a message, I am sure.

The message began many years earlier, on the night Juna

reached across the table and poked me in the stomach.

"Ouch," I said. "What was that for?"

Her poke had been a firm one, the kind you might use to wake a creature suspected dead.

"Your gut," laughed Juna. "It's expanded."

I looked down. She was right. My abdomen, which had previously been flat and muscular, now consisted of a bubble of flesh the size of a summer melon.

"Shit," I said and ran my hand over the swell. "What's this?"

I stood up and poked it too. Its density surprised me. It felt too hard and strange to be a part of me. Like a bag full of rocks. Like dirt packed down by many steps.

I looked at Juna, but she was still laughing.

"It's not funny," I said. "What the hell is this?"

"I don't know," Juna replied. "But look at your shirt."

I was wearing a grey t-shirt, a shrunk-down medium which had fit my old body with snug perfection. With this new form, though, the shirt couldn't reach the bottom of my stomach, which emerged from the space above my jeans like the hard-boiled egg of a giant.

Juna came over and lifted my shirt so that my midsection was exposed under the pale light of the kitchen.

"Can you feel this?" she said and flicked my belly-button, which had turned itself outward like a lonely wad of white gum.

"Yes."

"How about this?" she said and dug her nails into the place my ribs used to be.

"Of course."

Juna went down on both knees. She placed her hands on the sides of my gut and gave it a light squeeze. She massaged it with her thumbs, sliding downward in slow, measured strokes to where the gut disappeared into my still-normal-sized pelvis.

"What are you doing?" I asked.

"Be quiet," she said and pressed her ear against the gut.

"Do you hear something?"

"Just be quiet," she said, lowering her mouth to the gut.

Then Juna licked it. She licked it twice, actually. Why this happened I do not know. I only know that she was highly amused by what was happening and that her amusement was the only stabilizing force in the otherwise absurd situation.

"Okay," I said, backing away. "That's enough."

I walked back to our bedroom to find clothing that would fit me better. Juna followed. She flopped on the bed and watched me change. She never took her eyes off the gut.

"How do you feel?" she said.

"Fine," I answered, digging into the back of the closet, where I had stored an old extra large shirt that I had received as a gift for participating in a local 5K for charity.

"Nothing hurts?" she said.

"No."

"Nothing feels strange?"

"Not really."

This was the truth. From a physical standpoint, I felt completely normal. As such, I wanted to change shirts and proceed with the evening as if it were a normal night. I found the shirt I was looking for. It was just large enough to cover the gut.

"Let's just finish dinner," I said. "I'm not in the mood to talk about this."

"Of course," she said. "I'm sorry."

So we did just that. We finished dinner, split a red blend, watched a documentary on Shoeless Joe Jackson, brushed our teeth, flossed, made love, said goodnight, and got quiet. We completed these rituals in a normal manner and at a normal pace, never once mentioning the gut.

I was nearly asleep when Juna whispered, "Baby?"

"Yeah?"

"Can I ask you a question and you not get mad?"

"Yeah."

"You know that gut?"

"Sure."

"Where did it come from?"

By morning the gut had doubled in size. I noticed this before even getting out of bed. I no longer looked like a man hauling a summer melon in his midsection. I looked like a pregnant woman several weeks past her due date. I looked like the cartoon character who swallowed a beachball. I looked hilarious but also horrific—a monster trapped in a punchline.

Without waking Juna, I slipped out of bed and went into the bathroom. There I undressed and examined it. It was the strangest thing: nothing else about my body had changed. My face, my arms, my legs, even my cock and my ass—everything was still slim and muscular and regular. Only my stomach had changed.

There was a knock at the door. I opened it and let Juna in.

"Whoa," she said. "It got bigger."

"I know."

"Much bigger," she said and sat down on the toilet so that her face was level with my gut.

"I know."

"Can I touch it?" she asked.

"I guess."

When she touched it, she did so with great tenderness. As if applying aloe to sunburned skin, she lay her hands on the hardened globe and moved them in slow concentric circles.

"Does this hurt?" she said.

"Nope."

"Does it feel good?"

"Not really."

She grabbed my belly button, which was now utterly distended, and she rolled it between her thumb and forefinger like the knob of a radio. Then she turned me so as to examine the side of the gut.

"You have stretch marks," she said, tracing one of the several dozen pink snaking lines that now sprawled across my skin like a family of minor tributaries.

"I can see that."

"You want me to put some lotion on them?"

"No."

"That might help."

"I'm fine."

"You need to see a doctor," she said.

"I know."

"And you still have no idea how this happened? No theories?"

"No."

"Do you want to talk about it?"

"No."

"That's okay," she said, standing up. "But we are going to see a doctor."

Juna slapped my gut before leaving the bathroom to get dressed. The sound this produced was not the dull thud I expected, such as when you test a watermelon by thumping its yellowed underside. It was a hollow, metallic sound—the drop of a pebble into a dried up well; a coin in an empty cup.

Alone in the bathroom, I spoke a word into the mirror. I didn't aim it at the gut, though. I aimed it at my face. What I said (as I realized why this was happening) was this: "Monster."


We drove down to our doctor's office. After a brief time in the waiting room, during which we said nothing and watched a muted soccer match on the corner television, Dr. Honeycutt ushered us back to her office. For the next thirty minutes, Dr. Honeycutt performed a full inspection on my body. She took my blood pressure, listened to my heart, and probed my stomach with a blend of confidence and curiosity.

"Tell me about your daily diet and activity," Dr. Honeycutt said. "Particularly in the past 72 hours."

I told her the truth—that since losing my job as a sound

technician at our town's one recording studio, I'd been more active than ever; that every morning when Juna left for her law office, the first thing I did was complete a precise routine of stretching, running, and weight-lifting that totaled nearly two hours of exercise. I told her about my diet, which consisted mostly of green vegetables, fresh fruits, and the occasional lean meat.

"It appears you maintain a very healthy lifestyle," Dr. Honeycutt said.

She then placed her hands back on my stomach and began to press down at various places, all the while observing my face for some kind of reaction.

"And you're sure there's no pain?" Dr. Honeycutt asked. "Now's not the time to be a tough guy."

"I feel great," I said. "One-hundred percent normal."

This was the truth. Dr. Honeycutt appeared to believe me. She removed her hands and scribbled some notes onto her pad.

"Have you ever seen anything like this before?" Juna asked.

"Not quite this severe," Dr. Honeycutt answered. "But, yes. The stomach, or any organ for that matter, can swell well beyond its normal size."

"But why?" asked Juna.

"Any number of reasons," Dr. Honeycutt replied. "Physical or psychological."

"Psychological?" I asked. "Meaning what?"

"Stress, usually," she replied. "But also fear or anxiety or trauma. Has anything happened lately? Anything that might have triggered a significant psychological shift?"

"Nothing," was my answer to Dr. Honeycutt. "Absolutely nothing has happened."

Dr. Honeycutt nodded. She jotted more notes and told me I could put my clothes back on.

"Since you're not in any pain," she said. "Let's give it a couple of days. I want to see if the swelling will go down on its own. If not, we'll run some additional tests."

Over the course of the next week, the swelling did not go down. In fact, my gut got even bigger: melon to pregnant lady; pregnant lady to beach ball; and, eventually, to a size that made comparisons no longer salient. And though the gut itself grew, nothing else about it changed. Its density (still that of packed earth) remained the same. Its color (perfectly matching all other skin on my body) remained the same. There was discomfort but no pain; strangeness but no emergency.

On Juna's insistence, we saw six different doctors, including a world-renowned specialist from Johns Hopkins. All of them, however, arrived at the same conclusion. After admitting that mine was a severe case, they simply reiterated that, in terms of actual health, there were no major concerns. All of them echoed Dr. Honeycutt's theory—that the human body is a strange and stubborn machine; that things can and do happen for no apparent reason; and that the absence of pain was an auspicious sign.

"Contact us if anything changes," was the collective response. "Otherwise, continue your normal lifestyle and give the swelling time to go down."

Juna was remarkable through all of this. Not only did she take numerous days off work to drive me to the doctors' offices, she foresaw and prepared for all future changes: buying larger sizes of clothing before the gut reached its next size; installing various equipment in our bathrooms and showers so that I could still independently take care of my needs; and even reconfiguring our sex life so that, despite my new body, our intimacy remained strong.

I do not believe in making generalizations about relationships, unless the truth about a relationship cannot be accessed through other forms of specificity. Which is why, regarding my relationship with Juna, I don't mind saying that we were perfect for each other—truly perfect.

In saying this, however, I don't mean it as most people do. I don't mean that we found each other physically irresistible and that we enjoyed unfathomable sexual chemistry. I don't mean that our personalities were neatly aligned in terms of communication, idiosyncrasies, and humor. And I certainly don't mean that we felt "understood" or "known" by one another in some deep and spiritual way. In all of these ways, Juna and I were as imperfect as any other couple.

Instead, what I mean when I say that Juna and I were perfect for each other is that our pasts had shaped us into corresponding halves. She was the only child of two well-meaning but much older and ultimately distant parents. These circumstances combined with her shy disposition and her early love for books meant that she spent most of her childhood alone. By her own admission, she had no friends, no acquaintances, and no groups or teams through which she might know others and be known by others. Even her teenage job, which entailed proofreading instructional manuals for her uncle's electronics company, required absolute minimal human interaction.

"When I share this," she told me once. "People pity me. They assume that a child who is alone is necessarily lonely. But that was never the case with me. I never understood loneliness as something that needed to be fixed. In fact, I preferred it."

With the exception of one crucial variation, my story was almost identical. Like her, my parents were older when they started having children. They had me first and then, two years later, they had my brother. Although my parents provided us with all the basic forms of stability and provision, they were also distant and generally unaffectionate. My father worked a job that required constant travel and my mother worked a job that required no travel but enormous amounts of time and energy. Whereas Juna had used her long, quiet afternoons to read books, I used mine to play music, training myself on guitar, bass, harmonica, piano, drums, and even an antique dulcimer that my father had brought back from one of his business trips.

"Were you happy then?" Juna asked me, after I had described to her what it was like to spend so many hours alone in your room with nothing more than an instrument to keep you company.

I answered with complete honesty: "It was the happiest I've ever been."

As I said, however, there was one variation that distinguished our childhoods—and that was my brother's death. When he was two years old, my brother drowned in the bathtub of our home. My mother had been bathing him, as she did almost every night, when she suddenly received a phone call. Because my brother was a healthy two-year old, more than capable of being alone for a short spell, she left him in the bathtub and ran to her bedroom to answer the call. The call was from her boss, who did not typically call my mother at home but who, on that night, had an urgent matter to discuss.

No one knows for sure how long my mother was on the phone (although she later estimated it was somewhere between five and ten minutes). We only know that her boss's urgency caused her to temporarily forget about my brother and that, by the time she returned to the bathtub, he had drowned himself. She attempted to resuscitate him, as did the medics when they arrived. But it was no use. My brother was gone.

Following his death, many strange and unfortunate things happened. My father became increasingly stoic and remained that way until his own death, which happened in a freak plane crash, just several years after my brother's. To this day, I do not know how he dealt with what must have been unbearable amounts of grief. I know only that, from a child's perspective, a father who is absent and happy is not radically different from a father who is absent and grieving.

My mother navigated her grief in two ways—first through spiritual practices, then through pragmatic ones. Although I was young, I can still remember the variety of priests, psychics, and spiritual advisors that my mother would visit in order to have me anointed, prayed over, and protected.

"There is a curse against our house," she would say in those days, a theory doubly confirmed after my father's plane crash. "A curse that follows us like a dark cloud."

By the time I knew better than to believe in curses, she had moved on from paying strangers to recite prayers of protection to an apt combination of mood stabilizers, a razor-sharp grief counselor with a degree from Yale, and a new job in the field of real estate. She was healthier and, at least in the eyes of her introverted son, happier.

I have never asked my mother about my brother's death and, on the few occasions that she asked me what I remember, I told her the truth—that I was young, and that I don't recall much from that time. As years passed, she stopped speaking of the curse and, because of this silence, I assumed that, in time, she came to believe that it was lifted.

Before we were married, I shared all of this with Juna. Not only did I feel I owed her an honest view of my family history, but also I was interested to hear her interpretation.

"Who did your mother believe had cursed your family?" was the first question she asked after I had finished telling her the story.

"I don't know," I replied and trying (and failing) to think of a time when my mother had elaborated on her curse theory.

"God?"

"No."

"The universe?"

"No."

"Then who?"

"Her theory wasn't that specific," I admitted. "She was grieving and needed something to bear the weight of that grief."

"In other words," Juna said. "What was important was that she had some larger problem to fix, something to wrestle with regarding the future of her family."

I thought about this for a long time, so long in fact that Juna apologized if what she said seemed insensitive.

"It's not that," I said. "I'm just realizing, possibly for the first time, that I really don't know much about my mother. We love each other, but we're basically strangers."

I took a moment to consider if my evaluation had been too harsh. I could tell from Juna's face that she was saddened by this comment, which made me want to rescind it or at least clarify it. But as I sat there and thought about it, I was forced to admit that, by any normal measure of relationships, I was a stranger to my mother just as she was a stranger to me.

"It's true," I said. "I love her, but I don't know her. And although she would do anything in her power to support me, that does not mean she knows me."

Juna nodded at this, apparently appreciative of my honesty. Then, after a brief pause, she looked down and said, "Can I ask you one more question?"

"Sure," I said.

"Who does know you?"

Because, up until then, I had been honest, I decided to remain so for this question as well.

"No one," I said. "Not a single person on this earth."

"You want to know something?" she said. "No one here knows me either."

Six months later, we were married.


The gut was not the only strange thing that happened during that season of my life. My dreams also changed. They transformed from harmless synapse-collages into vivid and crystalline visions of flight. These dreams recurred on a nightly basis, no doubt as some kind of compensation for the fact that I spent my waking hours as a couchbound sloth. One week I dreamed I was a sparrow, flitting across the trees and rooftops of our neighborhood. The following week I found myself a hawk, larger and stronger, leaving our neighborhood to soar across county lines and return to the woods and rivers

I knew as a child.

After about a month of these flight dreams, I graduated from the bird family altogether and became a large black dragon, such as those I read about in high fantasy novels. As this beast I would sometimes opt for ascension, spiraling so high into the atmosphere that my neighborhood, my town, and eventually my state was relegated to a dim smudge, barely visible through the floor of clouds. In other dreams, I'd go no higher than my sparrow-self, sticking close to earth so as to burn everything in sight with the fire that spilled at will from my mouth. In these dreams, I'd burn and burn and burn, until everything green had turned to cinders as black and ugly as my dragon scales, until nothing was visible except for a barren wasteland of ash. These dreams gave me a visceral, albeit fleeting, sense of power, a feeling which snapped off like a light switch the moment I woke up.

In the waking hours, life moved forward at a steady clip. Never once, never a single time during any of this, did Juna ever complain, or criticize, or in any way indicate that we had turned a corner in our relationship and that her life was no longer what she had hoped it would be. She loved me as if everything was normal.

She loved me even after I asked her not to. Even after I asked her to leave.

"I'm a monster," I said to her one night, after we had tried and failed to have sex, on account of the gut. "I'm cursed is what I am."

"No, you're not," Juna said.

"Look at this thing," I said and punched my gut, which lay between us on the bed, a gruesome and uninvited guest.

"I'm looking," she said, tracing her fingertips over the same place I had punched.

"If you left," I said. "Nobody would blame you."

"I know that," Juna said.

"So do it," I said. "Leave."

"No."

That was when I asked the question I believed was at the heart of everything. I said, "This isn't going to get better. So what's the point of hanging on?"

What moved me most was how quickly she responded. It took her no time at all.

She said, "I don't want to fix you. I just want to love you."

This was another way in which Juna and I were radically different from each other—she was malleable and afraid of nothing, not even the future. These qualities may sound sentimental (and in some ways they were), but more than that, they were components of a carefully-constructed framework on Juna's part, one that she articulated shortly after I had shared with her my theory on being a constant stranger.

"I know why relationships don't last," she told me. "I've known since I was a kid. It's so perfectly obvious that I can't believe no one else sees it."

Assuming that I was aiding in the set up of some clever punchline, I looked over each shoulder in faux-paranoia and whispered, "Really? What's the secret?"

"There's an old Japanese proverb," she said. "It says, 'A man is whatever room he is in right now.'"

The look on her face suggested that this was not a joke, that she was advancing an idea that she truly believed in. As such, I tried my best to understand what she was saying.

"That sounds lovely," I said. "But what does it mean? And what does it have to do with why relationships fail?"

She bit her lip when I said this, as if considering a way to reframe her point.

"Let me ask you a question," she said. "Do you believe in identity?"

I thought about this. The question, both how it was worded and what it signified, sounded almost nonsensical to me. Did I believe in identity? I was not under the impression that one's identity could be believed in, or not believed in, any more than the fact of one's skin or skeleton could be affirmed or doubted. Though I was well aware of theories regarding cultural and social conditioning, I had never heard someone suggest an identity was anything less than a fixed fact at the core of what it meant to be human.

Sensing my confusion, Juna spoke up.

"Let me put it to you this way," she said. "I have this friend who is going through a divorce right now. I mention this friend because I recently spoke to her. We met for coffee not too long ago and she told me that she had left her husband. I'll admit that I was surprised. They were one of those couples that seemed so happy together. No one had the slightest suspicion that they were struggling."

"Appearances can be deceiving," I said, thinking of the many couples I knew who had a similar story.

"Don't misunderstand me," Juna said. "I love my friend dearly and support her decision to start a new life. But when I asked her why she was leaving him, she said something that I don't agree with. Something that proves what I'm trying to say about relationships and identity."

"What did she say?"

"She said she left him because he changed. She said that, when they first met, he was funny and charming and spontaneous, but that over the years he had become overly invested in his work and, by her standards, too serious about life. She said he was still faithful and ultimately loving, but that he had lost the spark that first attracted her. She said, 'I'm wired up for warmth and laughter. I'm wired up for fun.'"

"That's not the worst reason for getting out of a marriage."

"I see it differently."

"Are you saying your friend should've stuck it out?"

"Not necessarily. What I'm saying is that it seems unlikely that she, or anyone, is 'wired up' for one particular kind of love. I think we're far more flexible than we give ourselves credit for."

"Adaptation, in other words."

"Exactly," she said. "And I think the greatest threat to

that kind of adaptation is the belief that who we are and what we want is somehow fixed and immovable, that we have been 'wired up' for one particular thing. Maybe we are the opposite of all that. Maybe, like the proverb says, we are whatever room we're in."

Then, recalling our previous conversation, I replied, "So what you're saying is that we will always be strangers. Strangers, even, to ourselves."

"Exactly," she said. "And that being strangers is more a benefit than it is a detriment. We can learn to love anything or anyone. The only thing standing in the way of this love is the belief that we can't."

An entire summer passed with not a single change to my body. Then, on an otherwise uneventful Tuesday afternoon, when Juna was at work, and I was at home, a fortuitous intrusion occurred. I had fallen asleep on our couch and was in fact still sleeping when I heard the words, "Hey, you!"

The voice appeared to be coming from our television set. The problem being that I had not been watching television. And yet, when I ignored it, the same voice beckoned, "Hey! I'm talking to you!"

I opened my eyes and discovered that the television was inexplicably turned on, and that the voice belonged to the man on the screen. I sat up and checked to see if I had rolled over onto the remote control, activating the unit by accident. But the only remote we owned was exactly where I had left it, sitting on a table across the room. I ignored this minor miracle in order to give my attention to the strange man on the television.

He looked to me like one of those wizards out of the old storybooks. He had withered skin and long gray beard. He had a bent spine and bony fingers. Finally, he had an enormous hooked nose that signaled not only great wisdom but also intimacy with every secret you've ever been locked out of. All he lacked was a wooden staff and pointed hat.

This wizard was standing in a room that was both entirely white and entirely empty. Empty except for him and what he held in his hands: one brown leather suitcase.

"Time is running out!" the wizard said, undoing the clasps on the suitcase and spreading its halves to reveal several rows of small glass vials. Each vial had a label around its middle and a piece of cork for its top, like medicine jars from an old apothecary shop.

The man removed one of the vials and held it up in his gnarled, nut-brown hands. The camera zoomed in, so that the entire screen was dominated by the man's bearded face (now smiling) and the small glass vial, which I could now see contained a greenish-colored liquid.

"Time is running out," the wizard said again, "on this once-in-a-lifetime opportunity."

I noticed then, mainly because he was smiling as he talked, that the wizard's teeth were brown and viciously rotten. And yet he flashed them unabashedly, like two neglected rows of dirt-slicked pea gravel. Like fractious grubs writhing up out of the mud after having their home smashed by the boot of a bored child.

"What is it?" the wizard said, smiling right into the vial. "It's the cure for what ails you. Got a broken leg? You're cured. A curse you can't seem to shake? Cured. You name it, this guy right here has the dynamite to fix it."

Suddenly the camera zoomed back out and text appeared on the screen below the man. It was a phone number with an area code I had never before seen. It was also a price ($69.99) and a flashing red message ("Limited Time Only! While Supplies Last!").

I got up from the couch and retrieved the remote control. I was about to turn the television off when the wizard said, "I know what you're thinking, friend." And there was something about the way that he said this, something about the way he smiled, which inclined me to keep watching.

There was also that nose, which transported me back to

the faces of every wizard who spoke to me from those old and wonderful books. I listened until the commercial ended. Then, since there was nothing else to do, I called.

"Hello?" a voice answered, a voice which sounded exactly like the wizard's.

"Hello," I said. "I'm trying to reach—"

Here I stopped. It occurred to me that I had obtained precisely zero actual information from the commercial. What was the name of the product? Or, for that matter, the company? I was at a loss for words. An awkward silence stretched out across the line until, finally, the wizard spoke.

"I think I can help," he said. "You're calling because you're in trouble, is that right?"

"Yes, it is."

"You're calling because you've tried everything else. You've even tried the experts. Only nothing they offer has saved you? Is that right?"

"Yes, it is."

The voice laughed. For the second time I felt certain that this voice was the same voice as the commercial, that I was speaking with the wizard himself. I imagined that nose and it gave me great faith in whatever was about to transpire.

"Well then," he said. "You've called the right place."

"And what is this place?" I asked. "What is the name of your company?"

"Superfluous," he immediately replied.

"The name of your company is *Superfluous*?"

"No," he said and laughed again. "You learning our name is superfluous. That is, it is not necessary to complete this transaction."

"And what transaction is that?" I said.

"Your cure," the voice said. "Is that not why you called?"

I had to think about this for a moment. I did so while looking down at my gut. I had not weighed myself (doctor's recommendation), but I knew that I was close to three hundred pounds. I had almost forgotten what I looked like before the gut arrived. I had forgotten my old, original form.

"Yes," I said. "That's why I called. How does this work?"

The wizard explained the process and the process was simple. I send cash or check for the aforementioned price of $69.99 to an address he dictated (an address in South Dakota) and, after payment is received, the product would be shipped directly to my home address (which I provided upon request). The whole conversation took less than two minutes. Having jotted down all significant details, I thanked him for his time and advised that I would mail the payment immediately.

"One more thing," the wizard said, before I could get off the phone. "I feel compelled to warn you of potential side effects."

"Side effects?"

His voice lowered then slipped into a list not unlike those heard at the end of a pharmaceutical commercial. With a speed and rhythm that suggested he had delivered this script many times before, he ran down a list of side effects that included everything from diarrhea to skin irritation. So smoothly and quickly did he rattle off these conditions that I temporarily zoned out, nodding along until the final item, which was "hair loss."

"Hair loss?" I echoed. "Have many previous customers reported that?"

"No," he said. "Not many. For the most part, our customers are pleased with the effectiveness of our product. But it is our duty to give you the facts and let you decide what's right for you."

I thanked him, and he thanked me, and that was it. We hung up, and I mailed the money to the provided address, all but certain that I had just wasted $69.99 on a complete grift.

Two weeks later a small package arrived in the mail.

"Surprise, surprise," Juna said, having picked up the package on her way in from work.

"Is that what I think it is?" I said.

"Your cure," she said and cut open the package with a kitchen knife. "Compliments of Mr. Wizard."

That was what she had referred to him as ever since the first time I told the story. Her attitude towards him, and by extension his alleged cure, was the same impish optimism she applied to almost everything in life. When I told her what I had done and that I intended to try the remedy, she smiled and said, "What's the worse that can happen? Death? At least then you can say you got killed by a wizard."

We laughed at this and spent the next several minutes listing of all the ways you could die that were not half as awesome as being slain by a wizard.

"In all seriousness," she said, after we had exhausted the options. "I don't care what your stomach looks like. And I know you know that. I just wish you believed it."

"I do," I said. "But I'm getting tired of lugging this thing around. I'm ready for a change."

"If you're ready," she said. "Then I'm ready."

And from my spot on the couch I watched her remove from the box a small glass vial. It was identical to the ones on the commercial and was, like those, filled with a greenish-colored liquid. Juna removed the cork and sniffed the vial.

"What does it smell like?" I said.

"Nothing," she said. "It's scentless."

Juna turned the vial up, plugging the top with her thumb so that, once she turned it down, a small drop of the liquid remained on her fingertip. She sniffed the liquid again. Then she dabbed at it with her tongue.

"What's it taste like?" I said.

"Also nothing," she said.

Juna joined me on the couch, bringing the vial with her.

"As far as I can tell," she said and handed it to me. "It's water. Green-colored water."

I repeated the same process, inspecting the liquid in the light before smelling and tasting it. Juna was right. Whatever it was, it had no smell, no taste, and no significant clue to potential ingredients.

So I drank it. As with a shot of strong liquor, I brought the vial to my lips and poured the contents directly down my throat, exhaling immediately afterwards and waiting to see what, if anything, I felt. But what I felt was nothing. I felt the same as I had for months.

"Did they say how long it takes to work?" she asked.

"They said it takes effect almost immediately."

Juna used my gut as a pillow, which is something she did quite regularly during that time, adjusting her head so that she could look up into my face.

"Just in case," she said. "Do you have any last words?"

I could not think of anything clever. Suddenly tired down to my core, I could not even keep my eyes from closing. I put my arm around Juna, hugged her towards me, and fell asleep.

It was Juna's voice that woke me.

"Whoa!" she said.

"What?" I said, sitting bolt upright on the couch.

The pale light of the morning had flooded the room and Juna was standing over me, backlit by the sun. She had cupped her hands over her mouth and was staring down at me, vigorously shaking her head from side to side.

"What?" I said and stood up. "What is it?"

Then I saw the reason for her shock. I looked down at my gut. It was gone. The XXXL shirt I had fallen asleep in now fit me like an oversized dress. I tore it off and examined my stomach. There it was: my old stomach, my flat stomach, my stomach with hard muscles and smooth skin.

Juna came over and touched it. She flattened her palm against my muscles and ran her hand straight up to my chest.

"You're cured," she said.

"I'm cured," I repeated, dumbly.

"You're—" she said, her shock cutting short the thought. "You're *you*."

I could do nothing but nod and, like her, continue touching the once-familiar but now-alien flatness of my stomach. We did this, together, and then she kissed me. It was a violent and sincere event of a kiss. It was a kiss with so many emotions (joy and wonder and fear and gratefulness) all smashing into each other like wild unseen electrons. She ran her hands across my stomach and around to my back and up my spine where she pulled me to her.

"You're cured!" she shouted.

"I'm cured!" I echoed, half convinced that I was still dreaming.

Only I wasn't dreaming. It was real. Juna kept kissing me. And I kept kissing her. And there with the morning sunlight and my old body, we kissed, and I felt as if I had woken from a nightmare.

"How do you feel?" she said.

I ran a hand through my hair and prepared to answer, but before I could Juna let out a scream.

"What?" I said. "What is it?"

She didn't say anything. She didn't have to. I looked in my hands, which were overflowing with large piles of what appeared to be brown fur.

It took me longer than it should have to realize what was happening. I grabbed at my scalp and came up with the same thing: two large handfuls of my hair, not a single piece of which was still attached to my head.

When I stepped out of the shower, Juna and I stood in front of the mirror and surveyed the damage together. It was worse than we imagined. Although the gut had completely disappeared, my entire body was now bald and slick and sickening in the awful fluorescent light of the bathroom. Even my eyebrows and eyelashes had gone missing, small pinks strips of flesh now glistening like napping slugs in the place they once installed themselves.

Juna stood beside me and ran her hand over my head.

"Strange," she said, letting her hand fall down cheek and

across my chest.

"Yeah," I said.

"How does your stomach feel?"

"Good."

"Should I call Dr. Honeycutt?"

"No," I said. "They would interrogate me about the medicine. And I don't know what I'd tell them."

Juna asked if we could contact the wizard in order to make inquiries into the ingredients of the medicine.

"You still have that number in your phone," she said. "Let's call it."

It was true. I did still have the number in my phone. In terms of knowing more about what was in the medicine and what I might expect for my hair's restoration, I could not think of any other viable plans. We found the number and I dialed it.

Three times I called and each time the line rang for about two minutes before clicking over to an automated message. The voice on the message was not the same voice as before. It was a woman's voice and her language sounded like Spanish, which neither of us spoke.

With Juna's help, we wrote down the words from the message. Then, using an Internet translation service, we discovered that the language was actually Romanian and that the message said something to the effect of this: *Greetings and thank you for your call. We are sorry to have missed you. Due to operational complications, we are on temporary hiatus. Please try back in 6 to 8 months, at which time we will be happy to assist you with any questions you might have. Thank you and have a nice day.*

"Something's off here," said Juna, after we had translated, read over, and thought about the message.

Juna proceeded to compose a list of numerous logical concerns, any one of which probably should have occurred to me: that the message did not include a company name; that "operational complications" sounded vague and even suspect; that the message was in Romanian but the previous speaker spoke perfect English and the physical address was in South Dakota; and, finally, that just two weeks earlier this company had been running commercials and shipping orders.

"There is so much here that doesn't make sense," she said and listed about six more reasons that probably should have occurred to me before consuming tasteless, scentless liquid from an unknown company.

"Well there's nothing we can do about it now," I said. "I'll set up an appointment with Dr. Honeycutt and we'll move forward from there. At least the gut is gone, right?"

"Hold on," said Juna. "I have an idea."

She led me into the living room where she turned on the television.

"What channel were you watching when the commercial came on?" she said.

When I told her that I wasn't watching at all, that the television had been turned off, she thought about this for a moment then said, "*When* did the commercial come on?"

This I had to think about. In the several months I was afflicted with the gut, not only was I unemployed, I was seriously depressed. There came a certain point when the weight was so serious and the situation so dispiriting that I stopped all exercise and spent most of the day either in bed or killing time around the house. As a result, it was very hard to say whether the experience of seeing the wizard on television occurred at 10 A.M. or 4 P.M., since time for me during those months became largely inconsequential.

"I don't know," I admitted.

"Think," said Juna. "It was obviously after I left for work and before I came back."

"Sure," I said. "But that's a pretty big window."

"Didn't you say you mailed the money immediately afterwards?"

"I did."

"Well," she said. "When you went to the mailbox, had the mail come?"

"No," I replied. "The box was empty."

"Then we know it was before 2 P.M."

"Okay," I said, impressed with Juna's detective work but still not clear on how she intended to leverage it. "But what's your point?"

"My point," Juna said. "Is that if it happened once, it can happen again. We just have to recreate the circumstances under which it did."

It wasn't a full-proof point, but it was a point nonetheless. And I had nothing. So we talked about it and agreed, as Juna put it, "to recreate the circumstances under which it happened." Meaning that she hurried to get ready and left for work without so much as a cup of coffee. And that I remained exactly as I was and lay back down on the couch.

I closed my eyes and cleared my mind of all anxious or unnecessary thoughts. I steadied my breathing, inhaling deeply through my nose and releasing slowly through my mouth, imagining myself a dragon sending great plumes of fire into the air with each breath. Almost of their accord, my hands began to touch my stomach. Being hairless felt strange. But being freed from that gut and back to normal felt wonderful.

I continued this for some time: breathing and touching and, suspecting it might serve as a kind of invitation, conjuring up an image of the wizard and his suitcase. I could see his gnarled brown hands wrapped around one of those glass vials. I could see his two jumbled rows of rotting teeth, which reminded me of a friend but also of a wolf.

I was almost asleep when I heard his voice.

"Hey," he said. "Hey, you!"

I opened my eyes and there he was, holding his suitcase and smiling at me from my television screen like we were old friends. In the exact same sequence of gestures as the last time, the wizard removed one of the vials and held it up to the camera, which again zoomed in until the screen was filled with the wizard's face and the small bottle.

"Time is running out on this once-in-a-lifetime opportunity," the wizard said.

Again he smiled and again I cringed at his teeth.

"This is the stuff to cure what ails you," the wizard said. "Got a broken leg? It cures you. Got a curse you can't seem to shake? Still cures you. You name it, this little guy right here packs the dynamite to fix it."

This time, though, when the camera zoomed back out and text flashed on the screen, it was a different phone number. I copied it down and called immediately.

"You again," said a voice that sounded exactly like the wizard's. "We took care of you, did we not?"

"No," I said, and I explained everything that had happened: the gut's appearance; it's disappearance; the hair loss; the automated message in Romanian; and the circumstances under which I saw the commercial and called in.

When I had finished my story, the voice said, "I warned you about side effects, did I not?"

"Technically," I admitted. "But you could've been more clear on the severity."

"Feedback received," he said and laughed. "But you seem to have forgotten that, despite this one unfortunate side effect, the product perfectly fulfilled your desire."

I thought about this. And I had to hand it to him. On this point, the wizard was right.

"Thank you," I said. "I'll admit that I was skeptical, but your product did what none of the doctors and none of the specialists could do. It really did cure me."

"Yes, it did," he said. "But it appears you have a new problem, is that right? Does that mean you're in the market for a new cure?"

"Of course," I said. "As nice as it is to have my old stomach back, I can't walk around like this. I look like a freak. I don't even have eyelashes."

"That's nothing," he said, zero hesitation. "I have just the thing for it."

"What is it?" I asked.

"A cure, of course," he replied. "For baldness."

"Any side effects you want to warn me about?" I said.

"You're in luck there," he said. "Our cure for baldness has absolutely no side effects."

"None?"

"You heard me," he said. "It causes hair growth. That's it."

"So if I take it, I'll be cured?"

"Exactly."

"How much does it cost?" I said.

"How much would you like it to cost?" he replied.

"Is price negotiable?" I asked.

"Everything is negotiable," the wizard said. "*Everything.*"

I thought about this for a moment. But when I looked down at my arm, which looked without its hair like the pale and plastic limb of a mannequin, I became once again suspicious.

"There's a catch here," I said. "I just can't tell what it is."

"There is no catch."

"So you say. But how do I know this isn't another one of your tricks?"

"*Tricks?*" the wizard echoed, the word taking on a harsh, sinister quality in his repetition. "Now there's an ugly word. Why go and use a word like that?"

"My hair," I said, running a hand over my egg-slick scalp. "It's gone. My damn eyebrows are gone. Don't talk to me about ugliness."

"Unfortunate as that is," he said. "No one here is in the business of trickery. In fact, I seem to recall asking you if you had any questions. 'I'm good' were your exact words. So, do we have a deal?"

"We do," I replied. "I'll send the same amount. Tell me where to send it."

The wizard did not give me the address in South Dakota. He gave me one in New Mexico. And when I asked why this company appeared to be changing phone numbers and locations, he simply said, "Superfluous."

We hung up shortly afterwards. I sent him the money. A week later, a package with no return address arrived in our mailbox. Juna and I opened it together and discovered the same glass apothecary vial containing the same scentless, tasteless liquid.

"Drink it before we go to bed tonight," Juna said.

"Why?"

"That's how it worked last time," she said. "You don't mess with something that works."

When I woke up the next morning, I knew immediately that my hair had returned. Before climbing out from under the covers, even before opening my eyes, I could sense the distinct presence of hair on my head and chest and arms. And yet, I also knew that something was off. What I felt was undoubtedly hair; just not my hair.

Since Juna was still sleeping, I slipped out of bed and into the bathroom. I hit the light and what I saw, in many ways, was more shocking than the gut and even more shocking than the baldness. My entire body was covered in a hide of pure white hair. I looked at my body, which looked like a pale, furry body of an ape. I looked at my face, which stared back at me from the mirror like some sad and bleached-out werewolf.

"Fucking wizard," I grunted and imagined driving my furry fist into his hooked nose until every last bone was broken.

I had to do something before Juna saw me like this. So I filled the sink with hot water and lathered my face with massive globs of shaving cream. I tried my best to free some version of my old face. What made it hard, however, was how thoroughly all the white hairs had occupied my skin. They were everywhere, not just on my scalp and beard line but across my cheeks and forehead, over my ears, and completely flush to my lips and eye sockets. Even my nostrils brandished a light film of white fuzz.

I had not shaved half my face before Juna knocked on the

door. I told her to wait, but she insisted I let her in. Seeing no way around it, I opened the door. What happened then was strange and wonderful and calm. Juna came in and looked me over. She studied the white hair just as she had the gut and was not scared or shocked or even surprised.

"Okay," she mumbled repeatedly, circling me and continuing to run her hands over the fur. "Okay, then. At least now we know what we're dealing with."

"Which is?" I said, sincerely curious what Juna knew that I didn't.

"Equilibrium," she said.

"I don't follow."

"It's like in the old fairy tales," she said. "You have to read those stories in terms of equilibrium. Something happens to tip the scale one way. Something else happens to tip it back the other way. Magic can intrude and rearrange people's lives, but the fairytale begins level and it can't end until things are back at level."

"I see," I said. "First I lost the gut but got the baldness."

"Exactly," she said. "Now you lose the baldness but get this. They've got you on a scale."

"Okay," I said. "But who are they?"

"That's not the question," she said.

"What's the question?"

"The question is," she said. "If there's a scale, how do we get our thumb on it?"

Juna was right. The whole situation reeked of cosmic insincerity, of a childlike teeter-tottering of circumstance. We didn't need to play his game, only find a way to modify the rules of his game.

I looked back in the mirror. The person staring back at me, buried as he was beneath all that awful white fur, did not much resemble myself. Juna looked, too, and almost started to laugh. She licked her hand and slicked down a tuft on my shoulder that must have gotten spiked out in my sleep.

I hid for nearly two weeks. Once we learned that whatever hair we shaved off in the morning would grow back by lunch, we stopped shaving. As with the gut, we resigned ourselves to this new condition, at least until we hatched some salvation plan. I had been a circus freak once before in the form of a fat man, I could survive a bit longer in the role of wolf man.

It was a strange and lonely two weeks, Juna gone all day at her job, me killing the long hot days skulking around the house like a fugitive, desperate for sunlight and some kind of social interaction, but also horrified at what neighbors or friends would think if they saw me.

It did, however, give me time to think. And, in thinking, I began remembering. I played back all the conversations between me and the wizard, parsing each phrase and exchange for some clue. Eventually, I found what I was looking for. I remembered something he told me during my second conversation. He had said, "Everything is negotiable."

This gave me an idea. So I went to the couch and fell asleep. As before, I calmed my breathing and cleared my mind. I invited the wizard for a visit by conjuring up his nose and teeth just as I began to drift off to sleep. Then I heard it. Right on cue: "Hey, you!"

I opened my eyes and there he was. As he completed the same sales pitch as before, I wasted no time in calling the phone number on the screen. The voice that answered was his.

"Hello," he said. "How can I help you?"

"I'm calling with a question," I replied.

"Excellent," he said. "I'd be happy to assist you. What is your question?"

"Do you mean what you say?"

There was a pause after this. I could tell that the wizard had not expected this and, as a result, was thinking very carefully about his next words.

"Excuse me?" he eventually said.

"Your words," I rephrased. "Do they have meaning? Or are they simply sounds that fall out when you open your rotten mouth?"

The wizard laughed at this, as if to come off as amused. But he wasn't amused. He was uncomfortable and possibly even agitated. I was under his skin and we both knew it.

"If you have a concern about one of our products, then might I suggest you—"

"No," I interrupted. "Your products are incredible. Very effective, I must say. I'm not asking about your products, though. I'm asking about you."

The wizard was no longer laughing, and I could feel his anger through the phone.

"What is your question?" he said.

"You heard me," I replied. "I asked if you meant what you said."

"I'm sorry, sir," the wizard said. "But you're going to have to be more specific. What did I say and in what context did I say it?"

"You said that everything was negotiable. Those were your words. I want to know if you meant them."

To this the wizard took a very long time to respond, possibly upwards of a full minute. I said nothing during this time. I could sense that my question had put him in some kind of a bind. And I liked that. I liked feeling, for once, like I had some sense of power in our transaction. My thumb wasn't on the scale yet, but I was getting close.

"Yes," he eventually replied. "I said that and I meant that."

"Good," I said. "Then I'd like to negotiate something with you."

Following this, I told the wizard about my experience thus far with his products and explained that I was aware of the scale on which my life had been placed. And though I did not mention her explicitly, I advanced Juna's equilibrium argument, concluding my case by telling him that I was no longer interested in "the bullshit of cosmic back-and-forth."

"I want a cure," I said. "But not on those terms. I want to be made whole, but not on a scale."

"So much of what you said is true," he finally replied. "And yet so much of it misunderstands how healing works."

"Elaborate," I said.

"What you said about scales and equilibrium, it isn't wrong in terms of its recognition that actions have reactions. As you pointed out, when your stomach was healed, whatever power was called upon to complete that gesture, also triggered another release of power—a power that caused your hair to fall out. That part of the process is true. So I can see why you might understand it as a scale that constantly returns to equilibrium. But you're still missing a very crucial element."

"Do you have a better illustration?"

"I do," the wizard said. "You're not the first person to ask."

"I'm listening," I said. "Tell me how it works."

"Imagine this," he said. "You borrow a large sum of money from someone very important, someone with more power than you could ever dream of. You borrow the money because you need it and because this person is the only one willing to give it. You follow me so far?"

"I do."

"Now let's say, for simplicity's sake, that the amount you borrow is one million dollars. And let's say that this lender, the benevolent soul that he is, charges absolutely no interest. He gives you the money with one simple condition: that you pay it back in its full amount. If this was the case, how much money would you owe back?"

"One million dollars."

"Exactly. Now imagine that, having borrowed the money, you lose it. You lose every last penny. And, to make matters worse, you have no way of making more money, which is why you borrowed in the first place. Your earning power is zero and your debt is now one million dollars."

"Okay," I said, perfectly following the wizard's illustration but still having no idea where he was going with it or how it applied to the matter at hand.

"So now that we've established that part of the illustration, let me ask you this. If you can't pay what's owed, what is the lender going to do?"

"I don't know," I said. "Send someone to break your kneecaps. Kill you?"

The wizard laughed.

"You've seen too many movies," he said. "This is not that kind of a lender."

"Okay, then. I guess he'd seize assets, right? Repossess something of value."

"Exactly," the wizard said. "Since you can't pay what you borrowed, the lender is within his rights to take anything you have. This is the situation that you find yourself in. And in that sense, what you said about equilibrium holds partially true. Every collection that the lender makes brings the two of you closer to zero."

"Hold on, though," I interrupted. "So you mean to suggest that everything that's happened to me—the gut and the hair loss and now this ridiculous fur—is all part of paying back a debt that I owe?"

"Exactly."

"But I haven't borrowed anything. And who is the lender in this equation? God? Fate? The universe? There's too much here that doesn't make sense."

"All illustrations have their ambiguities," said the wizard. "But my purpose was not to make everything clear. The point was to help you understand what is happening and to illuminate the laws by which it functions. I don't know who the lender is anymore than you do. I don't know what it is that you owe or why the debt can't simply be forgiven. What I know is how it works. Everyone is born with a different debt, everyone is seized upon in a different way."

I thought about this horrific proposition. I thought about it in connection with me but also in connection with my brother and my father and the world at large. In one sense, it answered everything. In another, it answered nothing.

"So if I'm the borrower and the lender is some great mystery, who are you? What's your role in all of this?"

At this question, all of the tension left the wizard's voice. The tone he had used on the commercial, that of an old friend, returned. I could almost see his smile and great nose when he said, "Isn't that obvious, sir? We are the fixers."

"The fixers?"

"Yes," he said. "We didn't create the debt and we can't exactly forgive it. But we offer what help we can. That is why you called us, is it not? Because something awful had happened to you that no one else could fix? We're trying our best to fix it, sir, but there are elements at work here that are beyond our control."

The wizard's point settled into my thinking with the cozy inevitability of a math equation. I felt, or even knew, that there was no point in arguing with him. What remained to be negotiated had to be negotiated within this framework.

"I understand," I said.

"Did you still want to negotiate?" he asked.

"What's the point?" I said. "You just admitted that you can't forgive the debt."

"Forgive it? No. What we can try to do, however, is reconfigure it."

Although I was still listening to the wizard's words, by now my head was spinning and I was no longer following his logic. I looked down at my arm, at the snow-colored fur that now buried my skin. And I felt suddenly and thoroughly defeated. This is the way it would go: I would eek out my sad and low existence as a werewolf.

"I have to go," I said again and hung up without another word.

I lay back down on the couch and begged my mind for nothing more than the dream of the dragon. I closed my eyes and prayed I would wake up with a mouth full of fire. And when I did, I turned the waking world to ash, starting with the grass beneath my feet.

The next part of this story is hard to tell. How Juna came home from work and found me on the couch. How I told her about my conversation with the wizard and his explanation of what was happening. And how, looking back, I should have known better than to share with her what I did.

"But he did say that the debt could be reconfigured?" she asked, once I had finished recounting the entire conversation.

"He did."

"And he said that someone else could take on part of the debt?"

"He did."

"Did he explain how that process works?"

"He didn't," I said. "He might've, but I hung up."

I could tell from the way Juna was biting her lip that she was planning something, which is why I said what I said.

"Don't," I grunted. "Whatever you're thinking of doing, just don't."

She turned her face up to me, then. She looked hurt but also concerned. I apologized and tried to hold her. She pushed me away.

"You don't know what I'm thinking of doing," she replied. "And even if you did, what right do you have to tell me not to do it?"

"I'm sorry," I said. "You're correct about me not having the right to tell you what to do. But you're wrong about me not knowing what you're thinking. Because I know exactly what you're thinking."

"Oh, yeah? What am I thinking, then?"

"You're thinking you're going to save me," I said. "You're thinking that if this debt illustration is true, you're going to call the old guy yourself and arrange for you to take on part of what I owe. This is what you do. You're a fixer."

Juna said nothing. Then, because I felt I had to, I said

something I didn't believe, something that was horrible but that was also aimed at protecting her.

"Leave," I said. "Leave and don't look back."

"No," she said. "And that's not your call to make.."

"Look at me. Look at you. This is not what you signed up for."

"I didn't sign up for anything," she said. "I love you and I'm staying. It's that simple."

"If you won't leave, then I will."

Tears started to form in Juna's eyes. She tried to catch them before they fell, but they fell too quickly, rolling down in her cheeks and hitting our table in muted splashes.

"Why are you doing this?" she said.

The window for my leaving was closing. If I stayed, even for another minute, if I watched her cry and let her speak and went through the trouble of reasoning the whole thing out, I would know that she was right, that love was not easy and that it surely was not made up of saving someone from feeling the same pain as you.

Which is why I ran from that room as fast as I could. I ran out of that house and straight to my car, where I slipped in and drove off into the night, leaving behind my phone and my wallet and the only person who has ever loved me enough to take on the monstrosity of my debt. I drove until I couldn't anymore. Then I pulled over on the side of the highway and fell asleep.

The sunlight woke me. I sat up and looked around. Though illuminated by the morning sun, the highway was just as empty as it was when I fell asleep. I started the car but remained in park. I replayed the events of last night, recalling Juna's crying and my running off.

I continued thinking about these things, but something was wrong with my left eye. I rubbed it with my palm and pulled at its lid, suspecting that in the course of the night some tiny debris had intruded it. But no matter what I did to it, my left eye refused to work. Even stranger was the fact that my right eye worked just fine. Perfect vision there, where all the left one produced was an impenetrable gray-black gauze, like the darkened screen of a turned-off television. Like a city reduced to cinders.

Because of the shock of waking up in a car, and because of my left eye not working, it took me longer than it should've to look down at my body and realize that it was no longer covered in white fur. I looked at my hands. They were normal. I cranked down the rearview mirror and looked at my face. It was normal, too. I examined my stomach and my chest and my legs and everything down to my toes. No gut, no baldness, no fur. I was cured.

Except for the eye. And when I looked back in the rearview mirror, I saw why. My left eye was glazed and slightly discolored. Although some dim version of the iris and the pupil still showed, the entire eyeball was covered in a grayish film. It was at that moment, staring into that gray blind eye, that I knew the truth. Juna had called the wizard.

I drove home as fast as I could, the blind left eye providing its share of challenges. I made it, though, and stumbled into our house. I was too late. Juna—by which I mean not only Juna herself, but everything that had ever belonged to her—was gone.

Her disappearance was total. For months, I tried to locate her. I asked friends and family, all of whom claimed to know nothing. I hired the very best private detectives, but in the end, no one could provide even a basic clue as to where Juna had gone. Then the letters started coming.

What is she saying to me, here on Christmas morning, with her blind eye turned as such to the camera? Is she saying that, no matter what, we are bound together by the residual of that old magic? Or does she mean the other thing?

This, I think, is the only clue. While studying the card under the particularly good light of my kitchen, I notice a small black dot in the upper left hand corner of the side meant for text. It is ink. It is the place where she set down her pen and began to tell me something, before deciding that what I needed, or possibly what I deserved, was not something but nothing; not a cure, a curse.

# WHALE FALL

---

I.

If I could have climbed out of bed, I might have gone into work, but some days even the smallest movements are violence. So I called in, and I stayed in bed, and I stared at my phone for hours, clicking link after recommended link until an algorithm I will never understand led me to an article titled, "Humpback Whale Found Dead on Calvert Island." I read it. Grief can form such strange connections.

II.

I could not stop looking at the photograph of your body on the beach. Saddest was what the scavengers had done. The wolves who came out of the woods at night and ripped flesh from your sides. The eagles who bit chunks out of your back. It made me sick to see you like that, but I continued looking anyway. You crossed an ocean to get torn apart by strangers. The least I could do, alone in that apartment, missing all my recent dead, was to bear witness to your wounds.

III.

Even amidst the brutalities, there was a magic in the plain facts of your anatomy: your weight (sixty-thousand pounds), your color (gray as pavement after the rain), and your heart (which was the size of a bumper car).

IV.

The article said that usually when a whale dies, it sinks to the bottom of the ocean floor, where it begins to decompose, so as to feed an entire ecosystem of smaller creatures. Experts call this a whale fall.

V.

There is a clear kindness to nature's methods: the dead feed the living, who live on to feed the dead, all in a place too dark to ask why. Except that you refused such rhythms, and instead of falling, you moved forward. You sought land and light and us.

VI.

I do not believe you were trying to live forever. I think you were just trying not to sink.

VII.

You could not have known the immense value of your death. How once they found you on that beach, they would want your bones for a museum. How in order to get your bones, they would first need to empty you of everything else. Take note for the next time you think about dying on dry land: first they make you hollow, then they make their profit.

## VIII.

More pictures. Pictures of the scientists cutting you open and plundering your organs. They took anything that might prove useful for research, including your bumper car heart. Pictures of you being stuffed into a massive metal net and hung off a dock. Pictures of the cleaners that occupied your skeleton: crabs, shrimp, sea stars, snails, worms, and all varieties of fish.

## IX.

For one full year, you neither sunk down nor moved forward. You floated in a net hung from a dock, the opposite of empty: a home for hungry, wandering others.

## X.

When they lifted you out of the water, all manner of squatters spilled across the dock. Out came the crustaceans and isopods who had been living in your skull. Lodged along your vertebrae were not just barnacles and seaweed, but whole families of mussels, worms, and bryozoans. The last to crawl out were the pygmy rock crabs, who had spent the better half of a year crashing in the curvature of your ribs. They scuttled like fugitives for the water, while you waited in the light of the morning sun, empty as ever, waiting for the experts to decide what would happen next.

## XI.

Let me ask you this: after the wolves, and after the scientists, and after a year underwater bound in a net, did the warmth of the sun and the sound of so many voices grant you a certain faith in the future? I'm curious. I want to know how belief gets recovered in a place like this. I want to remember how to move.

XII.

The article ended with a link to a museum on Saltspring Island. I clicked on the link and was delivered to a brightly-colored advertisement. There you were, suspended above a crowd of children and soaked in the blues and pinks and greens of many unseen spotlights. The font at the top read, "Actual Whale Skeleton!" The children were smiling and pointing upwards in pure necrotic awe. A big red button appeared in the middle of my screen. It read "Click Here To Buy Tickets!"

XIII.

I thought about you all night, which was a strange kind of gift, since I don't sleep the way I used to. At some point, I stopped thinking about you, and I started talking to you. I told you what I would give to set things right. I told you how, even still, it was a dumb move to come to a place like this to die. Finally, I said, *If it's any consolation, I would've done the same. Anything, really, not to sink.* I waited all night for an answer, but it was morning before you finally talked back. *Get up*, you said. *Work.*

# LOCKJAW

We're building a ramp in the cut between our trailers. The wood we stole from the construction site doesn't match the wood we stole from school, but we don't care. It's summer and we're building something, me swinging the hammer, Tiny holding the nails.

"What's lockjaw?" Tiny asks, after we've finished and are deciding where to steal some paint.

"Who you been talking to?" I say, using a voice I learned from a late-night movie where one guy throws a knife straight into another guy's forehead.

"My mom," he says, using his real voice, which is a voice that wouldn't scare a hamster.

"You tell her about the house too?"

"Hell no," says Tiny, all scared now, shaking his head from side to side and making me think I should get all my voices from the things I watch at night.

"Then why was your mom talking about lockjaw?"

"Found a nail in my shoe."

"What are you doing with a nail in your shoe?"

"It was an accident. From yesterday, when we went to the house."

"Oh," I say, in my normal, non-movie voice.

"So what is it?"

"It's when you step on something rusty and get infected.

Does something to your blood and makes it so you can't move your mouth."

I flex my jaw to show him. "Like this," I say, through gnashed teeth.

Tiny makes his mouth like mine. Mutters "Really?" Bright blue eyes full of bright blue fear, he winces.

"Damn," he says and, releasing, rubs his throat. "Sounds awful."

"I've heard of worse," I say and, in some ways, am not lying.

"I haven't," says Tiny.

"Better watch out, then," I tell him, nudging the hammer against his sternum. "Better watch where you walk."


We hide the ramp and head to my house. We ditch our bikes in the yard and try to slip into the kitchen without my mother noticing. She does though and gets off the couch to interrogate Tiny.

"Where y'all going?" she says, fist on her hip, all pretending for his sake.

Tiny knows better than to lie to my mother. Sober, she can spot a lie regardless of what smoke it's wrapped in. Today, though, she's a far sight from sober. But since Tiny's too young to read eyes or figure what's in someone's cup, he stays scared and says nothing. Just chews on that bee-stung bottom lip that makes people in our trailer park ask who his father is.

"I said where y'all going?" she repeats, phantom tough because she too has seen her share of movies.

Shooting Tiny a "Watch this" wink, I step in between them and looking her dead in her watery eyes say, "They're about to play ghost tag down in the cul-de-sac."

"Alright then," she says and looks around the living room for her cigarettes. "Y'all be safe."

With her back on the couch, we grab what we need from the pantry and bust out the back-door. While walking towards our bikes, I reach my hand down into my pocket. Even though I know it's there, I like to touch my Swiss Army knife. Something about cold, hard metal sitting in your hand and feeling like a promise.

Outside, Tiny spits through his teeth like I taught him and says "That was close."

"Don't worry, man. I got your back," I say, which is something else I got from that movie with the knife-throwing hero.

"And I have yours too," says Tiny. "We're not late, are we?"

"Come on," I say, and ride towards the construction site, Tiny breathing hard behind me.


We use the binoculars to make sure the bum is still there. The grass around the construction site is gold and overgrown and, except for the house he's in, there's no buildings around. Of course he's there: right where we left him yesterday, slumped on that half-built porch with his empty cans of beer and Glad-bag full of nothings.

For Tiny's sake, I scan the ground for anything with a nail sticking out of it.

"Do you see him?" Tiny asks.

"To the East," I say, nodding towards the backside of the development.

I say East and Tiny looks impressed, but I've been turned around ever since Miss Torwalt taught us moss only grows on the North side of trees and the sun sets in the West. I doubt Miss Torwalt has ever been to our trailer park, where the trees have moss on all sides and the sun goes down a different place each night.

We share the binoculars. From back on the ridge, the bum doesn't look like much. It's when we get right up on him that we see the hair like bleach-white seaweed stretched over his scalp. We see the pink skin splotched with mud-colored freckles. Right up on him, we see the red eyes. Albino was the word the encyclopedia gave to it and since I looked at plenty of pictures the night before I'm not half as scared as Tiny, who has no choice but to fear the unfamiliar since his mom can't afford decent literature.

"Bring it here," barks the bum, standing up when we're still twenty feet away.

Tiny falls in behind me, and I'm waiting to feel a tug on my shirt the way he used to when we'd sneak into Old Man Frazier's junkyard and mess with his goat, or when we'd climb on Miss Jameson's grill to peek into her bathroom window. He used to twist the ends of my shirts into little handles for him to hold onto and when things got bad it felt like I was dragging him. He doesn't grab it, though, and I'm tempted to turn around and let him know I 'm proud of how far he's come. "Courage comes in degrees," was something my father used to say, and I see the point is not without its application.

Ten feet out the bum charges us. Tiny grabs me. I grab the knife inside my pocket. The backpack with the food falls to the ground.

"Relax," the bum says, snatching the backpack off the ground and returning to his spot on the porch.

Fingers wrapped around the knife, I imagine throwing it, picking as my target a large beige mole on his neck. I envision the blade leaving my hand and sliding into his flesh easy as a coin into a slot.

"Where's the magazine?" says Tiny.

"About that," he says and tells us a story about getting rolled.

Watching his brown mouth deliver the narrative, I think about what my father used to say about excuses, about how they're like assholes because everybody has them and they always stink. If I didn't care about being original, I would've repeated his saying word for word. But Tiny's spent too much time around my father and I'm trying to teach him to find his own voice. It doesn't do to spend your whole life repackaging other people's best riffs.

So what I say is, "We held up our end of the deal," then look back to make sure Tiny's good. And he is.

"You little pervs will get your mag. Just need more time is all."

Tiny sniffs the air loud enough for us all to notice and then, after hesitating for a moment, says, "Y'all smell that?"

In unison, the bum and I inhale, attempting to catch the scent in question. But before either of us can process the alleged scent, Tiny sneers and says, "Smells like bullshit to me."

Out shoots my palm. Tiny slaps it. By degrees, Old Son.

"I know," the bum says and looks halfway sincere in his shame. "And I'm sorry."

"When then?" says Tiny, still talking with his new gall and largeness.

"Day after tomorrow. Swear I'll have it."

He sticks out his filthy hand in Tiny's direction. Tiny though, instead of shaking it, turns on his heel and says over his shoulder, "Damn right you will."

I don't let go of the knife until we're back up on the ridge and peddling towards home. Every so often I turn around to make sure Tiny is behind me. And he is.

Back home, Tiny asks if I can come over. His mother is fixing breakfast-for-supper, which means scrambling eggs and soaking blueberry muffins in melted butter before dropping them in the Fry Daddy.

"I'm game," I say. "And given the task at hand, we might as well make it a sleepover."

When Tiny looks confused, I spell it out for him: how we'll sneak out and go back to the house; how we'll see first-hand what the bum is hiding in his trash-bag; how if we don't return with our magazine, we'll damn sure find something to tip the scales back to our side.

Tiny says nothing after this. Just nods his heads, bites his lip. All that courage he had back at the construction site is gone, ditched at the door like our muddy shoes.

"What?" I say. "Are you scared that we're going to get caught?"

Tiny nods.

"Listen," I say, knife-thrower's voice in full effect. "That bum couldn't catch a cold."

Miracle of miracles: the line, my father's, works. Out shoots Tiny's hand. I slap it and for some reason, repeat the line. "That bum couldn't catch a cold."

We laugh.

Later, after Tiny's mother has passed out, we slip out the back door and ride down to the ridge. Thirty feet back is a streetlamp, but its light doesn't reach the construction site. The darkness below us is different than the one behind us. And we know it. Crouched down and saying nothing, we both silently consider the best way to go home without seeming like a coward. We know from the movies what happens to cowards.

"How do we know he's down there?" whispers Tiny, his face so close to mine that I can smell the blueberries on his breath.

"Where else is he gonna go?" I whisper back and, because it seems like the right thing to do, reach into my pocket and pull out the Swiss Army knife.

"Here," I say and lay it in Tiny's hand. "Just in case."

"Okay," he says and holds it in his hand like a wounded bird.

Tiny flicks out the large blade. What few stars still hang above us make it shine like the straight white teeth of a familiar smile. I watch Tiny rub his thumb along the edge. I watch him snap it back in place and stand up taller than before.

"Don't worry," I whisper, leading the way down the hill. "We'll be back before you know it."

Yesterday's rain has left the mud just wet enough to give off a sharp smacking sound as we tiptoe to the edge of the porch. Our steps stick, not enough to lose a shoe, but enough to slow us down and make some noise. He's snoring as a drunk will, but still we stop every so often to make sure he's going steady. And he is. Steady drunk and sleeping right beside the bag.

I'm knifeless but carrying a dollar store flashlight. Tiny's right behind me, twisting the bottom of my shirt into a handle. His hand is trembling. I almost tell him to go wait for me on the ridge. Then I remember the Swiss Army knife and say nothing. I take the step in front of me and conjure a vision of Tiny, courage complete, spinning through the air and gutting the bum. Old Tiny, bad as a late-night movie.

My mind's eye is on fire with Tiny's victory when the plank beneath my foot lets out a moan so loud my thumb twitches and actually flicks on the light. Paralyzed, we watch as a beam of light finds and frames the bum's face. Tiny lets out a whimper and flings himself off the porch. I begin to backpedal, but by some sick trick of gravity the light stays trained on the face and, falling backwards, I am forced to watch his eyes like two tiny flaming discs snap open. Tiny screams, and I drop the flashlight, and the bum rises to his feet, and we turn to run, and I am gone. Tiny is screaming, and I am gone. In all that vile darkness behind me, the smack of mud and muffled voices blend, but I do not know what is happening. I do not know a thing. Screaming fills my ears, and I am gone, gone, gone.

I run through the dark until I'm home, and the door's locked, and I am looking at my mother's face, bathed as it is in the blue glow of the television. I am nearly crying when I wake her.

"What?" says my mother, sitting up and rubbing her eyes. "What is it?"

"I had a bad dream," I lie and collapse into her outstretched arms.

By the time I collect myself and go to the window that looks out on Tiny's house, his porch light is on, but his bike is nowhere I can see. I think about going back out, at least to check his house if not to return to the construction site.

And I'm on the verge of doing so before my mother calls me into the living room and starts firing off questions about what happened. It's just sweet tea in her cup tonight so it takes a good half hour to set her straight.

By the time I return to the window, Tiny's bike is lying on his lawn.

I don't dream that night because I don't sleep. It's those eyes that keep me up. The eyes and the screams. I imagine the knife-throwing hero is standing watch by my window, and I catch a quick nap before morning.

The next morning I go over to Tiny's house. His mother opens the door. Her smile says she doesn't know. Then she tells me he's in his room. When I open his door, Tiny's still in bed, staring up at the ceiling where he has stuck about a dozen of those glow-in-the-dark stars in the shape of a smiley face. He does not look away from the stars when I come in.

"Hey buddy," I say and pat the bottom of his foot.

"Hey," Tiny says, quiet but distant, like an echo down a hall or a voice from one room over.

"Last night was kind of wild," I say and sit on the edge of the bed.

"Yep," Tiny says, louder but still distant, still faded and far off sounding.

He still hasn't looked at me. His body is stiff, arms arranged straight down along his sides, legs unbent and neatly outstretched. His mouth has a tight quality and as I notice these things I begin to think about the time between me getting home and me seeing Tiny's bike. I look around the room for the Swiss Army knife and see no sign of it. I can't bring myself to ask him about it.

Instead, I say, "That old bum chase you very far?"

"Nope," whimpers Tiny and shakes his head from side to side.

"So you got away clean, huh?" I say, forcing a laugh.

Tiny doesn't answer right away. He opens his mouth as if he means to say one thing, but then, as if something catches the words before he can release them, says nothing. Just swallows hard. Finally, with that small unmoving mouth, he whispers, "Yeah, I got away clean."

When it becomes clear Tiny isn't going to say anything else, I get up.

"See you around, then," I say and hold out my hand for him to slap.

He doesn't, though. He stares at the stars on his ceiling and no longer seems to know that I'm in the room. Just lays there and breathes. And then I'm not in the room. I'm outside, walking towards my house and thinking of what the knife-thrower would say. But the best movie line I come up with isn't good enough. Not even close.

# A FOREST DARK AND DEEP

I was at the Fourth of July barbeque when I saw him. I can't explain it. I looked up and there he was.

I wasn't ready. I had my wife and kid with me. We were sitting on a blanket on the lawn behind the neighborhood pool. There were cheeseburgers and ice cream and beer. We were surrounded by neighbors and friends. Like everyone else there, we were watching the sky get dark so the fireworks could begin.

Sutton, my two-year old, had climbed into my lap. He was eating vanilla ice cream from a cone, but instead of licking it, he attacked it in small, vicious bites. I held him and for his sake pretended to be present. I would've been present—except for this man.

He was alone and standing at a distance from the crowd. He was holding a cheeseburger that had been thoroughly covered in ketchup. Only he wasn't eating it. He was just standing there and looking up at the sky as if something had been written there that only he could read. My wife must have caught me looking at him.

"Do you know that man?" she asked.

"No," I said. "I don't believe I do."

Sutton was still biting his ice cream. His bites had made it lopsided, so much so that the white blob was starting to slide off the cone. He would have lost it had I not saved it. I brought the whole thing to my mouth and licked the leaning side, providing momentary stability.

I did this then looked over at my wife. But she wasn't looking at me. Now she was looking at the man.

"I've never seen him before," she said, licking her own ice cream, which was peach. "Have you?"

"No," I said.

I looked at my son. His blob was in trouble again. I considered saving it.

"You think he's someone's guest?" my wife asked.

"Must be," I said.

He still hadn't touched his hamburger. He just held it like a useless weapon. He stood under the purple sky like the statue of some general who used to be important.

I closed my eyes and tried to forget him. I heard a man's voice say it would be another hour before they started the fireworks. I heard a woman's voice offer my wife a beer. Then Sutton flinched and something cold plopped into my crotch.

"Everything's fine," I said, letting the blob fall to the grass and lifting Sutton into my arms. "We'll get a new one."

I continued holding Sutton on the walk to the ice cream stand. He pressed his sticky cheeks into mine. I rubbed my hand in circles on his back. All this while keeping my eyes on D. I had, by then, stopped denying that it was D. It didn't matter that it had been seven years since I had seen him, or that he had no feasible reason to be here. It was D. And I couldn't see D. without remembering Corrine, my first wife.

Corrine and I met at the College of Charleston, where we both majored in education. We graduated in Spring, found teaching jobs in the same district, and married within the year. We then bought a yellow house on James Island and rescued a lab named Doughnut who would join us for evening walks on Folly Beach. This season of life—the one with the yellow house and the beach and Doughnut, the one I could not imagine getting any better than it already was—was the same one from which I made one of the worst decisions of my life.

Although I was entirely happy with Corrine, I cheated on her, executing a brief affair with a woman at my job. Imogene was this woman's name. Like me, Imogene was young and recently married. Also like me, she was completely in love with her spouse. Because of this last fact, we were both surprised that a trip to Florida to attend a conference on standardized testing could serve as an occasion for the sudden breaking of sincere vows.

"I love Noah," was one of the first things Imogene said to me, not five minutes after the first time we had sex. "I would never leave him."

We were on the small bed of a bad room at a Holiday Inn in Tampa, where we had retreated for drinks after a day of lectures and workshops. I still cannot recall the exact point in time when we transitioned from drinking to kissing, much less from kissing to sex. I can recall many things, even something as small as the fact that Imogene's breath always smelled like lavender, but how things unfolded the way they did was a mystery.

"I know how this looks," Imogene said. "But Noah is my soulmate. You have to believe me."

"I do," I replied. "Corrine's everything to me."

We stayed up late that night. We continued drinking and talked about many things, mainly how what we had done felt unique. Our understanding of an affair—which we admitted having gleaned from television and hearsay—was fixed in the idea of deprivation. Married people cheated because of some commodity they craved but could not find in their spouse. Affairs were, when you got down to it, searches. Yet we agreed that, for us, searching had nothing to do with it.

"Noah's incredible," she said. "Funny, smart, kind. And whenever we do decide to have kids, he's going to be the best dad ever."

"I believe you," I said, eager to validate her cheerful assessment of their life together.

"And I don't know for sure," she said. "But I don't think he's ever cheated on me. What I mean to say is, given his character, I don't think he ever would."

I replied with similar things about Corrine and meant them in all sincerity. Corrine was also funny, smart, and kind. Corrine also had character and, to my knowledge, had always honored our vows. It felt odd but good to celebrate our spouses in this way. It felt like speaking the truth over the strange aftermath of a vivid dream.

And yet, laying there in the dark and defending our spouses, we felt the need to submit at least one salient explanation for why we had done what we had done. It wasn't easy. On the one extreme, you had categories like "accident" and "mistake," neither of which were entirely accurate. On the other end, though, were theories that assumed levels of plotting and desire which seemed too high, too drastic for our situation.

"Happy people can cheat," she said and meant the words to be declarative, except that, on the final word ("cheat"), her voice went down in volume and up in pitch, casting the comment as a question.

She cleared her throat and tried again.

"Cheating doesn't mean that your marriage is in trouble," she said, steady this time in volume and pitch. "It's possible that cheating doesn't mean anything at all, and that we shouldn't even call it cheating. We should call it what it is—an incident."

Not long after this remark, we quit theorizing. We started kissing again and, again, I wondered how it was possible for someone's mouth to taste so much like lavender. I asked her, but she just laughed and kept kissing me. Then we drank more, fucked more, took a shower, and fell asleep watching television.

Morning came and, when it did, Imogene and I agreed

that whatever had happened had simply happened—two happily married people crossed paths at a conference and had, for reasons that may or may not become clear in the future, tried something new together. It was a memory like any other memory and, in time, it could come to mean as much or as little as we wanted it to.

We left Tampa two days later with the understanding that it would never happen again and, as such, that there was no need to tell our spouses. We agreed we would not tell anyone what had happened nor even acknowledge it between ourselves. We agreed we would act as if it had not happened because, in a certain sense, it had not.

Why we broke this agreement, I cannot say. But after returning to Charleston and setting back into our routines, we continued sleeping together. We met at least once a week, our spouses' work schedules providing windows of time so large and convenient that it barely felt like sneaking around. We fucked in my home, we fucked in her home, and once during a professional development day while the rest of the teachers enjoyed a catered lunch, we fucked in the backseat of her SUV.

Not that it matters, and not that we ever held to it, but every single time we slept together, we swore it would be the last time.

"I can't keep doing this to Noah," Imogene would say. "I love him. I really, really love him."

"I know," I would reply, meaning every word. "I'm the same way."

Despite the fact that Corrine knew nothing about my affair with Imogene, I could not rid myself of the feeling that everything between us had changed, that we had crossed over some kind of a threshold, even as, in many ways, the plain surfaces of our marriage were as good as they had ever been. What I sensed but could not say was that our life together had been inscribed with a kind of darkness. Our attitudes and our voices and our chemistry and, inexplicably, even our bodies—these things no longer contained their old light. Ever since my decision to continue the affair, we seemed, the both of us, not like our old and true selves, but like two shadows who had been hired to stand in as replacements.

Unable to share this feeling with either Imogene or Corrine, I retreated into my own thoughts, and, as usual, my thoughts retreated into metaphor. I thought of the fairytales I used to read as a kid, the ones where the characters start out in one place, then they cross through some kind of doorway, and suddenly they are in a different place. Back then, I liked the beginnings of those stories the best, since they always opened up in little sun-lit villages where everything seemed perfect. Everything seemed perfect until the character decided to leave home and travel into some dark forest, sometimes because they needed something, but usually just because all the light and goodness of the village had left them wrecked with curiosity. They always made it back home, but not without having seen a bit of hell out in the darkness.

What scared me most was not the idea that Corrine and I had stumbled through a door into a darkness neither of us understood and only one of us even saw. What scared me most was a question. What if, unlike the old stories, the door you pass through is one that closes behind you? What if, in reality, even if you want to return home, there comes a time when the door is locked and return is impossible?


It was much darker by the time we got a new ice cream and returned to our blanket. It was not exactly night but close. I put my son down and he began to eat his cone, this time with exaggerated tenderness. I sat down too and stole a glance at D. He was no longer standing still. His cheeseburger was gone and he was smoking a cigarette. He was walking towards the parking lot.

"Come here," my wife said.

She was sitting crossed-legged on the blanket, facing the place where fireworks would soon fill the sky. She was rubbing the tops of her thighs, gesturing for me to lay my head in her lap. I thought about this. But then I looked at D. He was almost to the parking lot.

"Actually," I said and stood up. "I need to run a quick errand."

My wife looked at me then as she had every right to—like it was both strange and suspect that a man who had never once used the expression "run an errand" would leverage it, of all times, in the middle of a Fourth of July barbeque. When she asked if it was necessary, I told her it was. When she asked me where I was going, I said I would be right back.

Who knows why she let this pass. I had not expected she would. I had expected, and even secretly hoped, that she would question it and insist on my staying. When she didn't, when she smiled at me and said, "Okay," it felt as if the choice had been made for me.

I looked past my wife and found D. in the parking lot. He had unlocked the door to the most decrepit Chrysler LeBaron I had ever seen. The LeBaron had craters of rust on all sides. It had a t-shirt stuffed in the gas tank. D. flicked his cigarette onto the pavement and climbed inside.

Before leaving, I kissed Sutton on the top of his head. Then I leaned down to kiss my wife. Her mouth, still tethered to the present, touched me in the place above my cheek but below my eye. Her breath smelled like sugar. This should've tethered me, too. This should've done so many things.

When D. pulled out of the subdivision, I followed. I didn't know where he was going, but I was right behind him.

The affair with Imogene was disorienting for the both of us. We swung so rapidly from lust to shame and back again that we didn't know if we were getting what we wanted or doing what we hated. We wanted to stop but didn't and struggled to understand our ambivalence. We talked about it, as we had that first night, but came up with nothing.

It's possible that thrill had something to do with it, that despite the love we had for our spouses, we were not yet ready to surrender the inner electricity that comes from illicit love. It's also possible that, even though our marriages offered happiness, we had suddenly developed an appetite for something quite different from happiness, something whose name we didn't yet know. Whatever the reason, the affair lasted nearly four months, until one day after school when Imogene came into my classroom and locked the door behind her.

"It's over," she whispered. "For real this time. I had a long talk with Noah last night. I told him everything."

After saying this, she began to cry. She held her face in her hands and trembled. I sat there at my desk and thought of what to say. I sensed there were at least a dozen questions worth asking. Except not one of them came to mind, and, as she stood there waiting for me to say something, I said nothing.

Eventually I blurted out, "Are you okay?"

"I'm fine," she said, drying her tears with her palm. "But it's not me you should be worried about."

That night I told Corrine everything. I expected one of several things to happen. She would be devastated and ask me to leave our home until she had set conditions for my return. Or she would be devastated and ask me to leave our home and, in time, rule out all conditions for return, a short separation leading to a clean divorce. This felt like the most likely option, given how willfully I had deceived her. Or, in a final future, Corrine would be devastated but not ask me to leave our home, which was the option I most wanted but also most feared, since her presence would become both a window and a mirror—a window through which I could view her pain but also a mirror in which I had to face the ghoul who caused it.

Except that none of that happened. On the night I told Corrine everything, she listened to the entire story—from the Holiday Inn in Tampa to Imogene's confession in my classroom—and, when there was nothing left to share, she looked me straight in the eyes and said, "Finally."

"Finally?" I echoed, too stunned to say anything more intelligent.

"Yes," she said. "It's about damn time."

I fell, at this moment, into some kind of low-level shock. My scalp tingled, the room went askew, and it felt like I had stumbled through some portal in reality and ended up in a dream state. Because not only had Corrine said "It's about damn time," but she was smiling. Her eyes were smiling, and her mouth was smiling, and every inch of her skin and muscle in her body appeared to be smiling. Truly smiling.

"It's funny," she said and took my face in her hands. "I always knew you were hiding something. Damn it feels good to have the masks peeled back."

"Masks?" I stuttered. "Baby, what are you talking about?"

Following this, she kissed me on the lips. Then she pulled me into an embrace. It was, all of it, too strange. I had to pull away from her. I had to stand up and ask her what was going on.

"Relax," she said and looked at me as if I was being needlessly dramatic. "I realize you were expecting a traditional lashing, but I can't fake it any longer. The truth is, I'm glad you're finally being honest with me. Because there's something I've been dying to get off my chest. There's something I really want to try."

I was stunned and must have looked it. Corrine reached out for my hand and pressed it between both of hers.

"Listen to me, baby," she said. "You are not in trouble. You are fine. We are fine. Can't you see that this is a good thing?"

I studied Corrine's eyes for some sign that she was pretending or, possibly, that she too was in shock. But what I saw was not just her normal look of kindness and love, but the sense that nothing had even happened, that what I had just confessed was tantamount to "I forgot to pick up the drycleaning." I looked for hurt, but there was no hurt to see.

Her eyes, her body, even her breathing—everything about Corrine corroborated her unequivocal message of "This is a good thing."

Still holding my hand, Corrine led me to the couch, where we sat down and faced each other. She was still smiling and I had, by then, no idea what was about to happen. On some level, I suspected that the next thing she would say would be the thing she had been dying to get off her chest. But I was wrong. What happened was she told me a story.

I followed D. out of the neighborhood. I followed him down the mostly residential street of Old Spartanburg, then I followed him onto Pelham, where we sat at two different red lights before merging onto the interstate. I did not worry that he would see me. It was dark and, despite it being a holiday, there were plenty of other drivers on the road.

We drove south, away from the Greenville I knew, towards poorer and less familiar towns, towns that might be Mauldin, Simpsonville, or even Fountain Inn, depending on how far D. intended to go. He drove in the right lane at a speed that was well under the limit. I matched it perfectly, keeping a hundred feet between us as an extra measure of security.

We had been driving for around ten minutes and had already passed the exit for Mauldin, when I arrived at that point where it is suddenly necessary to either fully commit to the plan at hand or else scrap it altogether. I was, given how reckless the whole situation was, leaning towards the scrap option. But just as I thought this, the cherry flicker of D.'s turn signal announced his intention to get off at the next exit.

Did I, even once during this time, consider calling my wife? About every seven seconds. I hated not calling. I hated thinking of her and our son, back there in Sugar Creek, sitting there on the blanket and waiting for fireworks without me. I hated how unstable the whole thing felt. Had I been able to explain what I was doing or what I was after, I might've at least attempted a conversation. But since I would not have known how to answer even the simplest of her questions and since that (the not answering) seemed to me more frightening than the not calling, I didn't call. Instead I vowed to tell my wife everything I knew as soon as I knew it.

D. pulled off at an exit that had a number (25) but not a name. It was a dark road leading to a dark town, and I knew that I had never before had a reason to be here and thus, logically, never had. It had one sign, indicating that to the left was a 24-hour gas station. D. turned left and made for the gas station. I followed.

"You remember Liam?" Corrine said.

I didn't and admitted it, after which Corrine reminded me that Liam was her boyfriend during her freshman year of college.

"Liam lived in one of those all-male dorms," she said. "Shoeboxes, we called them. Little gray rooms just big enough for two beds, two desks, and some posters."

I nodded, having lived in a similar dorm my freshman year.

"This was the semester I was rooming with that crazy Baptist girl from Tennessee. So when it came to Liam and I going somewhere to mess around, my dorm was off-limits."

"Okay," I said, having heard several stories about the girl from Tennessee.

"Liam had a roommate, too," she continued. "This guy they called Ogre."

"Ogre?" I said, certain that I had never heard any stories about a guy named Ogre.

"Yeah," Corrine said. "That wasn't his real name. But that's what Liam called him. And, to be honest, he did kind of look like one."

"He looked like an ogre?" I said, still unclear what this had to do with my affair and yet, in all honesty, suddenly fascinated by what this might mean.

I wanted to ask more questions about Ogre, but Corrine continued without elaborating.

"Whenever Liam and I messed around," she said. "We would try to be discreet. Ogre had evening classes, so that made things pretty easy. But occasionally I would spend the night at his shoebox. And, as you know, when you mess around in a room that size, it doesn't leave much to the imagination."

I said nothing and, after a brief pause, Corrine continued her story.

"Some time went by like that. Until this one night, Liam sits me down and tells me there's this thing he's always wanted to try."

Corrine nodded at me and I nodded back, entirely unclear about the basis for our nodding.

"And I liked this," Corrine said. "I liked that he respected me enough to be honest. But, at the same time, I could tell he was embarrassed. It was like pulling teeth to get him to tell me what it was."

"What was it?"

"He wanted to watch me," she said. "With Ogre."

Because it was dark and I was tired, but also because we had never before talked like this, I wasn't sure I understood what Corrine was saying. I asked her to clarify. Before replying, she took my hand and placed it on her left breast. Her heart was beating at a slightly faster pace. Her nipple had already stiffened.

"He wanted Ogre to fuck me," she said. "And he wanted to be in the room while it happened. To watch us."

She then removed my hand from her breast and moved it to her neck. She closed my fingers around her windpipe and asked if I was okay. I was and told her so.

"Just finish your story," I said.

"Liam had already talked to Ogre," she said. "The two of them had worked the whole thing out. He just needed to know if I was okay with it."

When, after several seconds, Corrine had not said any-thing, I intervened and said, "Were you?"

"Yes," she said. "I was."

Again Corrine fell silent. We sat there in the darkness for a long time without saying anything. She was still holding my hand to her neck and I could feel her breathing.

"When you think about that," she finally said. "How does that make you feel?"

"I'm okay," I said. "Surprised but okay."

"Jealous?" she said and kissed my ear.

"No," I replied, which was a small part of the truth.

"Disgusted?" she said, moving down to my neck.

"No," I replied, which was a small part of a lie.

"I can give you details," she whispered. "If you want them."

"No," I said. "I'm not jealous and I'm not turned off. But that's different from being curious."

After this, she started back on her story. She started tell-ing me about times and schedules. I stopped her.

"Corrine," I said.

"Yeah?"

"Ask what you want to ask," I said. "Ask me anything."

When I said this, Corrine removed my hand from her neck. She then lowered her mouth to my stomach and kissed me directly on my navel. It was a strange kiss, slow and hard. It felt as if she was trying to push something out of her lips and through my skin. She said nothing the entire time she did this.

"Just ask it," I said.

Corrine would arrive at her question, but not before more context. With her head still down on my stomach, she told me about a website she had found. She said it was a website for "locals with alternative lifestyles." She told me about a message board and some of the posts she had read. Then she told me about the post she had published just several days earlier.

"You want someone to watch us?" I said.

"No," she replied. "The other way."

I had to think about this for a moment before realizing what she was asking.

"Oh," I said. "You want me to watch?"

"I do," she said. "But only if that's what you want. If it's not, then tell me now and this conversation will be over."

Never in a million lifetimes would I have come up with an idea like this. And yet, she had. She had come up with it, conducted research on it, and waited for what she felt was the right time to be honest about it. It would be a lie to say that, there in our bed, with Corrine waiting for my answer, I did not think about what I had done with Imogene, did not on some level think about strange things such as darkness and doorways and how certain motions of love can never be reversed and barely be explained. And yet, it was not that simple. I was thinking about what Corrine was asking and what I had done, and I was thinking about many more things too. Whatever I was thinking, when I spoke, I said, "Tell me more."

When I said this, I could feel Corrine's mouth lift itself into a smile against my stomach.

She told me more. She told me about the strangers (mostly men but also a few women) who had responded to her message. She told me about her process for narrowing down the interested parties and, ultimately, for choosing a "bull." When I asked her if that word meant what I thought it meant, she told me it did. Then she told me about D.

"D. would be the bull," she said. "And you would be the cuck. He fucks me. And you—"

Here Corrine stopped, almost as if she wanted me, not her, to finish the thought. I complied.

"He fucks you and I watch. Is that right?"

"Yes," she said. "Hypothetically."

"Of course," I said. "Hypothetically."

"I wanted to do some research before I asked you. But everything I've read says that the only way this works is if both partners are one-hundred percent on board. And I want you to take all the time you need to think about it. I don't care if you need— "

"I don't need time to think about it," I interrupted. "I can give you my answer right now."

Corrine lifted her head off my stomach. She sat up and stared directly into my face. She was holding her breath.

"My answer is yes," I said.

As with the first time, her hands found my wrists and pinned them down. We made love in this position and, afterwards, we lay there and started to fall asleep. But before we did, she said one more thing.

"There's something I need for you to say," she said. "And it's not enough for me to know it. I need to actually hear you say it."

"Okay," I said. "What is it?"

"Say that you are free," she said. "Free to speak your mind. Free to tell me no."

I could and I did. I told her I was free to stop this anytime I wanted.

From my parked car, I watched D. walk towards the gas station. I watched the slow rhythm with which he swung his large arms as he walked. I watched the muscles of his quads and his hamstrings and his glutes, all visible and shifting under his jean shorts. I watched the way he licked his lips and the way he dragged his feet and the way his already tanned skin shifted into an even darker shade as he passed under the weak fluorescent lights. He entered the station. I lit a cigarette and stayed where I was.

Inside there was one clerk and several other men. On his way to the refrigerators that lined the back wall, D. greeted them like old friends. They smiled and said something to him. He smiled and said something back. Then he opened one of the refrigerators and removed two large cans of beer.

I noticed that he did not pause to search for these particular beers or to compare their price with other products. I wondered if *this* purchase at *this* time at *this* location was, for him, a nightly ritual.

Then I wondered what I had wondered many times since first seeing him: what on earth was he doing at Sugar Creek's Fourth of July barbeque? For this I had nothing, not a single viable answer for why, after so many years, our paths would cross at that place and at that time.

Holding the beers in one hand, D. walked towards the register and, on the way, plucked from the rack a large bag of chips. As with the beers, there was no hesitation. D. then set all three items on the counter and began conversing with the clerk, who appeared in no hurry to scan the merchandise and request payment.

Then my phone rang. It was my wife, and I sent the call to voicemail. She called again. I sent that one to voicemail too. She sent me a message: *Are you okay?* I replied: *I am. But it's taking longer than I thought.* She said: *Where are you?* I replied: *Did I miss the fireworks?* She said: *No. But they are about to start. Where are you?* I replied: *I am almost finished. Not much longer.*

My wife sent me several more messages after this. They were reasonable, caring messages that expressed healthy measures of concern. I did not read them, however, until much later. What I did, after telling her that I was almost finished, was turn my phone on silent and slide it down into my pocket.

I looked up in time to see D. walking out of the station. Again I watched him. I watched him walk towards the LeBaron. I watched him stop and remove his phone from his pocket and lick his lips and say something to his caller. Then I watched his large white teeth gleam as he smiled at whatever his caller's reply had been.

He pulled out of the station and drove down a dark road with nothing but woods on both sides. I emptied my mind of all thoughts: of my wife, of my son, of Corrine, of everything. I imagined my mind was a small box containing absolutely nothing and I continued, unphased, to follow the dim lights of D.'s car through more miles of darkness.

Because we were both teachers, Corrine and I loved the holidays. We loved the long breaks. And since we did not work second jobs, did not have children together, and did not pursue any hobbies that required travel, we typically spent our breaks at home. We would stay up at night to watch television then sleep in as late as we wanted. During the afternoons, we did whatever we felt inclined to do at any given moment, often leaving the house on a whim to try a new restaurant or make a day trip to Savannah. But, more often than not, we would spend the entire day lounging around the house in sweatpants, doing nothing and wanting nothing more than what we had.

It was during one such break (Christmas, to be exact) that Corrine asked me a question. It was a question that either had everything or nothing to do with what Imogene and I had done. We were on the couch, having just finished pizza and a bottle of white wine, when she straddled my chest and pinned down both of my arms.

"Tell me something," Corrine said.

"What?" I replied.

"What are you holding back from me?"

Confident but not certain that I understood her meaning, I asked, "As in sexually?"

This didn't warrant an answer. Only an eye roll from Corrine, followed by a smile and her tightening grip on my wrists.

"Yes, sexually," she said, pressing more of her weight onto my chest. "Tell me what you're holding back."

I say she had me pinned me down, but Corrine was four feet and eleven inches tall. She weighed ninety-two pounds and had the slender hands of a child. She wore elementary teacher glasses and elementary teacher jewelry and had little mud-colored elementary teacher freckles scattered across her nose and cheeks. Combine this with her kinked orange hair, her high-pitched voice, and the slight gap between her two front teeth and you had, to my eyes, the world's most beautiful woman.

"There's nothing to tell," I said and pretended to struggle under her grip. "You know all my stuff."

She looked down at me and shook her head.

"I don't believe you," she said.

"It's true," I replied.

Then, still holding me by the wrists, she said, "You can't think of a single thing that you've always wanted to try?"

I wanted so badly to have an exciting answer for this. Because I could tell from her face that she expected it, I wanted to confess something dark and thrilling. But the truth was, I had nothing like that in me. I loved Corrine, I loved our sex life, and I had never, not even once, held anything back or wished we could try something different.

Because I was still constantly thinking about it in those days, I considered the possibility that this question had something to do with my affair. I thought about telling her, as I had before, that sex with Imogene had not only not been better than sex with her—it had been worse. Worse foreplay, worse talk, worse positions, and worse orgasms. In fact, towards the end of the affair, there were several times when I, while in the act with Imogene, imagined it was Corrine I was with.

But because none of this seemed appropriate to share, what I said was the closest thing to the truth that I had in me.

"What can I say?" I told her. "You're perfect."

Corrine sighed, clearly disappointed, and released me. She said, "You're perfect, too," after which we kissed, made love, and lay quietly in the dark until we both fell asleep. I was not a fool. I knew what she had extended to me. It was a moment in which transformation was momentarily possible. Moreover, I knew that I had squandered it with my lack of imagination. I knew all of that when I answered. But if you have made a plan to no longer lie to the people you love, you are not left with many options.

In the long and lazy holiday break that followed, Corrine continued circling back to the topic of fantasies. Once more she asked me what I was "holding back," and twice she asked about my "secrets." When it became clear that I could not provide a satisfying answer to this prompt, she widened her inquiry to more sprawling questions about sex. She asked about my early sexual experiences. After I described them, she asked for more details. She wanted to know what the girls were like, what I was like, what we did and how it made me feel. She asked me what kind of porn I'd watched and how it made me feel after I had looked at it. She even asked me about sex with her: my favorite thing about her body, my least favorite thing about her body, and if I had ever masturbated to a particular sexual memory of her.

"Where is this coming from?" I asked her several times.

"Nowhere," she would always reply. "I'm just curious."

This was not the truth, although neither was it a lie. This was one of the numerous and necessary veneers some people need to manage certain desires. This was a peeling back of those veneers, slowly and sequentially, so that when the time was right to speak the truth, we would both be ready.

I remember the night the truth came out. I remember we had just finished dinner. I was getting ready for bed, standing in front of our bathroom mirror and flossing my teeth. Corrine came into the bathroom and hugged me from behind. I remember looking in the mirror and how, except for her small freckled arms wrapped around my stomach, my body completely eclipsed hers.

"I want to ask you something," she said, still just two small arms around my stomach. "And before I ask it, I want you to know that you are free to say no."

"Okay," I said and continued flossing.

I wanted to look at her while we spoke, so I attempted to unclasp her hands and move her beside me. She squeezed tighter, though, so tight that I gave up and assumed there was a reason she wanted to stay hidden from my sight. I assumed that this too was a necessary veneer.

"What I want to ask you," she said. "Is to *try* something."

While tailing D. down a mostly desolate stretch of highway, an image began to form in my mind. It was not the image of a door. It was the image of a window. It was a window I imagined would be at the house where D. eventually arrived. This window could have looked into a kitchen or into a living room or even into a bedroom. None of that mattered. What mattered was that this window would separate the light inside from the dark outside, and that I would stand in that outer dark and press first my fingers then my hands and eventually my face against its glass. When D. got where he was going, he would park his car and go inside. I would park mine and find this window. I became convinced that this is how it was supposed to happen. Because what mattered was this: that I could watch and that in watching him I would receive some kind of answer to the question that had begun to take shape in my mind.

Corrine had done her research. The night before our first time with D., she sat me down at our kitchen table and, as if preparing for a very important business meeting, read from a printed document which contained a bulleted list of all conceivable rules, conditions, and expectations. Almost as soon as she began, I saw that something had changed in her. The night she had told the story about Liam and Ogre, she had gradually inched her way towards the request. She had been timid, even fearful. I remembered how, at first, she could not even look at me as we talked.

Now, though, all fear was gone. Not only was she calm and confident, she was professional. As she moved down the bulleted items on her document—when D. would arrive (6 o'clock sharp); what she would be wearing when he did (black silk dress, nothing underneath); what they would do before having sex (spaghetti dinner, red wine); what I would do while they did this (listen from our bedroom); the place where they would have sex (our bed); the place where I would watch (our closet); the lengthy and non-negotiable restrictions on my involvement (zero interference and absolute silence, even if addressed); and, finally, a FAQ for successfully navigating the time before, during, and after the session—Corrine spoke with the cold unflinching confidence of an expert.

When she had finished, she asked me if I had any questions. I asked the only one that came to mind.

"Why the closet?" I said.

Corrine, still in the mode of a professional, allowed her mouth only a slight twist towards a smile.

"For one," she said. "Because that's where I've decided to put you."

"Oh," I said and recalled something she had said in a previous conversation, something about how the most important factor was "control"—me relinquishing mine; D. relinquishing his; and Corrine using the both of us as "instruments" for her pleasure.

"For two," she said. "Because this is about agony."

"Agony?"

"Yes," she said. "I want you to want what you can't have. And I want you to watch what you can't stop."

"And that's what this is about?" I said. "That's what turns you on?"

"That's part of it," she said and kissed me on the mouth.

She did not ask me, at this time, if the idea of agony turned me on. It didn't. But somehow that didn't matter. Like a man who has gone through hunger pangs and emerged on the other side to feel (shockingly) no longer hungry, I had passed through some kind of threshold with respect to my own sexual appetite. I didn't want to be turned on. Corrine took care of that. What I wanted in this situation was for her to be happy.

About a half hour before D. arrived, Corrine advised me that, effective immediately, I had lost the privilege of speech and would thereafter remain absolutely silent. She demanded I nod to indicate understanding. I did. She then stripped my clothing one piece at a time and led me to the closet in our bedroom, where she instructed me to sit down on the ground. I obeyed.

"I'm going to get ready for D.," she said, beginning to strip off her own clothes. "And you are going to sit here and watch. Do you understand?"

From the floor, I looked up and nodded.

"Good," she said and moved the sliding door of our closet until it was nearly closed.

When she did this, darkness filled the closet and, except for the column of light created by the crack in the door, which was an inch or maybe less, I could see nothing. I could see only a section of our bedroom wall and one corner of our mattress. For several minutes, I sat there in the darkness and said nothing. I stared at that corner of the mattress, studying the pattern of silhouetted flowers on our sheets. I did this until Corrine's face appeared. She was, I could tell, completely naked.

"This one sliver," she said, running her fingers up and down the column of light. "Is all you're allowed. Do you understand?"

I nodded and, for what felt like a full minute, Corrine's face floated above me in the light. I could not tell if she was smiling, but her voice, though firm, sounded as happy as I had heard it in months.

She left me there and I said nothing. I said nothing until it was all over, until after listening to them eat dinner at our table, and listening to them move from our table to our bed, and after listening to Corrine walk D. to the door and say goodbye and shower and change and brush her teeth and, finally, after what seemed like an eternity, return to the closet to release me.

What do I remember from that night? Mostly the sounds. I remember hearing Corrine and thinking how she sounded like someone suddenly flung into a state of extreme pleasure but also slight pain. Also I remember the brief glimpse of the one body part my sliver permitted. It was D.'s hand. He had, after Corrine mounted him, flopped back on the bed so that the flesh of his hand rested, palm upwards, on the corner of our mattress. This was all I saw of D. that night, and I remember how, when it wasn't touching my wife, that hand lay there on the bed like a large bird of prey poised to take flight.

In the years that followed this season in our marriage, people who heard what happened have asked me, "How could you do that?" By people, I mean men. Such men have a curiosity that is based equally in disgust and curiosity. What they mean to say by asking "How could you do that?" is either "How could you do that to a person you love? To your own wife?" Or, more likely: "How could she do that to you? On what planet is an arrangement such as that considered anything close to love?"

These are not easy questions, but I attempt them anyway.

I say to such men, "Do you love your wife?"

To which they always answer, "Yes."

Then I say, "And because of that love are you compelled to make certain sacrifices? To do things you wouldn't otherwise do?"

All of these men, regardless of race or region or class or anything else, answer this question as if having studied the same script: "Of course. But that's different."

They are so confident and articulate for most of this conversation, but here, at the point that really matters, no one can find the words. Here, when I ask them what makes their sacrifices different from my sacrifices, no one yet has given me the reason. What is wrong with these exchanges? Is it the question or the answer? Their imagination or mine? I cannot for the life of me tell which.

So fixed was I on my image of the window that when D. pulled over to the side of the road, I didn't know what to do. The place which he had stopped appeared to be nothing more than an empty field surrounded on all sides by dark woods. I looked in every direction and saw not a single structure, much less a house. And yet, that was where D. pulled over and parked, turning off his car completely.

Although I had left plenty of space between us, there was no point in continuing to pretend like I was not following him. It was possible he had been aware of me since Sugar Creek and had lured me to this exact location for a confrontation. Or, for all I knew, the road we were on had no outlet and by driving past him, I would hit a dead end and have to face him on my way out. My options dwindled to two: either perform a sharp u-turn and hightail it home; or pull over alongside him and let whatever was meant to happen happen.

I thought about my wife and son, which made me want to pursue option number one. But then I thought about the questions I had carried for so many years, questions that existed even if I didn't know the way to turn them into words. That must have been my problem—thinking.

So I parked my car behind his. I killed the engine and sat in the dark of my cab. As far as I could tell, D. was doing the same thing. I stared at the back of the LeBaron and waited for something to happen. During this time I tried again to empty my mind of all thoughts. I tried not to think about the fact that what I was doing was at the very least unhinged and likely dangerous. I tried not to think about my wife, who had probably continued sending messages to my phone even after I silenced it. I wanted my mind to become an empty box so that whatever happened next would establish itself as the sole content.

But I failed in this. I watched as D. climbed out of his car and started walking towards mine, and as I did, my mind was not empty but full. It was full with the light of too many memories from too disparate times—my son's lopsided ice cream, a man who looked like an ogre, a woman with breath that smelled like lavender, closets and slivers, mirrors and boxes, my new wife at home wondering where I was, my old wife in Charleston with our yellow house and Doughnut, all of it smashing together in my head in some queer convergence of particles while D. stood outside my window in dark of the night and used a hand I'd seen before to knock three times.

I rolled down my window and looked up into his face, ready even then to receive some kind of answer.

We hosted D. another four or five times at our home on James Island. This took place over the course of a month or so. And, as best as I could tell from our closet and through my sliver, each visit went about the same. D. would arrive at six o'clock sharp. Corrine would invite him inside to a dinner that had already been prepared and was waiting on the table. They would eat and drink and talk and engage in various forms of minor foreplay. Then they would migrate back to the bedroom, where, without casting so much as a glance in the direction of the closet, they would fall on the bed and finish what they had started.

The ritual afterwards was equally unchanging. After D. and Corrine had finished, Corrine would escort him to the front door and issue a farewell that was either too brief or too soft for me to hear. Then she would return to our room, take a long hot shower, and complete her entire pre-sleep routine before coming to the closet and opening the door. Even then she would not speak in her normal voice but in the firm imperatives designed specifically for such nights.

"Get up," she would say. "Get on the bed."

To which I would nod and comply.

Once on the bed, Corrine, still using her dominant voice, would initiate a strange but meticulous routine of touching me while asking simple yes-no questions, all of which shared the aim of describing what her and D. had just done.

"Did it hurt you when D. pulled my hair?" she might

ask, while massaging my calves. "Did it hurt you to hear me scream?"

Nod.

"Did it hurt you to hear what I begged him for?" she might ask, moving up to my thighs. "Did it kill you that you couldn't see him do it?"

Nod, nod.

This would continue, her caresses increasing in intensity only after her questions had increased in specificity and filth. Eventually, when she was ready, Corrine would climb on top of me and continue this ritual of inquiry until we had both finished. Only after that, and after a long spell of silence in the darkness of our bedroom, would she face me and speak once more in her normal voice.

"Be completely honest with me," she might say, nothing so much as a pause to suggest that a stranger had just come into her home and fucked her while her husband hid in the closet. "How would you feel about going to the farmer's market this weekend?"

"Sure," I might say. "That sounds like fun."

To which, in her old voice and with her old mouth, she might kiss me and say before going to sleep, "Remind me, if you can, to pick up some kale."

It went on like this for a month or so. It would have gone on for longer, had Corrine not suggested a change. Instead of me in the closet, witnessing through my sliver, she pitched a scenario where D. would come to our house just as he had in the past, and the two of them would eat and drink and go into the bedroom just as they had in the past, but the new difference was that I would no longer be present.

What Corrine wanted was for me to check into a hotel room and wait for her to call. When she called, I was to pick up and listen. I was to pick up and listen for as long as they allowed me. Additionally, instead of D. leaving immediately after sex, he was going to start spending the night. I could return home the following morning, at which time D. would be gone and everything would be back in its old state.

"Why?" I asked, only once. "Why are we suddenly chang-ing things?"

"Because I've seen you in that closet," she said. "And I don't think you're really hurting."

We tried the new arrangement for several weeks, at which point Corrine suggested another change. Now she wanted to leave our home and meet D. (and possibly several other men). They would meet in an undisclosed location, do whatever they wanted to do for as long as they wanted to do it, and remain out until they felt like coming home.

"This is the ultimate agony," she said. "You don't get to see what's happening. You don't get to hear what's happening. It's one-hundred percent imagination."

Before agreeing to this new set up, I asked her, as I always did, if this was what she wanted. She told me it was. And she asked me, as she always did, to tell her that I was free to say stop this at anytime. I told her I was. And when, after I said it, my mind did not reel with the reasons I wasn't okay with any of what was happening, I considered the possibility that this was love—the gradual forgetting of what you used to want, so that someone else can have their happiness. I thought about fairytales and considered the possibility that, when the door through which you entered the forest has locked behind you, the only way out is to turn your back on where you came from and to push deeper into the darkness.

We talked over the details and agreed we would try it for the first time on the coming Friday. Corrine would leave our home right after dinner, she would meet D., I would spend the night alone, and in the morning, we would reconvene. That was the plan.

Except that Corrine did not come back.

For the first two days, I figured it was an improvisation. And as I called her phone and got no answer, and as I stayed up both Saturday night and Sunday night to watch the street outside our home, I could almost hear her voice in my head, explaining her logic: "I wanted to see how long I could stretch it out. I wanted to know how far I could take you."

I figured Corrine would come back and that I would tell her what I had known for some time—that this whole arrangement had gotten out of control; that it was my fault and I was sorry; that although in my twisted mind I had imagined it would get us out of the dark forest, it was clearly only making us more lost.

I never got the chance to say any of this. After that Friday night, I never saw or heard from Corrine again.

When I rolled down my window, D. lowered himself to it. In an effort to better see me, he stuck his entire head into my car, bringing his face so close to mine that I could smell the chips and the beer on his breath. So close I could see tiny white stubble exploding in patches out of his chin and upper lip. We stayed like that for several brutally uncomfortable seconds: me staring at him; him staring at me; neither one of us saying a word. It was D. who eventually broke the silence.

"You Garcia's guy?" he said.

"No," I said and bracketed the urge to ask him who Garcia was.

Hearing this, D. pulled back but only slightly. His head was outside my car, but he was still holding onto the frame of my window and staring into the cab. He seemed bigger, much bigger than I remembered, both in height and weight. Although, because of Corrine's sliver policy, this was the first time I had ever looked at him straight on.

It was then that I looked down at his hand— *really* looked—and what I saw sent a chill through me. It was not, as I expected it to be, the same hand I saw through the sliver, the hand I had carried in my memory with piercing clarity for the last seven years. This was a different hand. This hand was missing the tops of its two smallest fingers. And though I considered the possibility that this was D. and that some kind of accident had occurred since our shared time in Charleston,

I also considered the possibility that this wasn't D. at all but a stranger. I saw no way out except to ask.

"What is your name?" I said.

At this he pulled back completely, removing his hand from the frame and nearly (but not quite) balling it into a fist.

"My name?" he said. "Why do you want my name?"

"Is it D.?" I asked. "Is that what you went by? About seven years ago, in Charleston?"

Without taking his eyes off me, he considered this. And as he did, I thought of how the two of us would have looked to someone driving by at that exact moment—two men locked in confrontation on the Fourth of July and in the middle of nowhere.

"If you don't work for Garcia," he said. "Who do you work for?"

"Nobody," I said. "This is isn't a work thing. I just need to know if your name is D."

He whispered something under his breath when I said this and continued staring at me. His face, which was masked by the darkness outside, could've meant a mix of curiosity and anger, or it could've meant anger alone. Either way, I sensed he was deciding what his next move would be. To make it easier, I spoke.

"I followed you," I said. "Because I thought I knew you."

I was waiting for either a confirmation or a denial, but instead he gestured with his hand and said, in a strangely calm voice, "Get out of the car."

"No," I said, having become convinced by then that I was mistaken and this man, whoever he was, was not D. and had not a single answer to my questions.

"Get out of the car," he said, slowly this time and with the threat of violence saturating every word.

"There's no need," I said. "I'm clearly mistaken."

I started to say more, but before I could, he mumbled something under his breath (something that sounded like "Fuck this shit") and walked back towards his car. Why, when everything in me insisted that this man was not D., I got out of my car and followed him as if he was D., I cannot say. It's possible I wanted, or needed, to believe this.

"Okay," I said, catching him right before he got into the LeBaron. "I'm here."

He turned and faced me. Though I was standing still, he took two large steps so that he was directly in front of me. At this distance, the difference in our sizes became vicious. He was six inches taller than me and at least fifty pounds heavier. If this interaction became suddenly violent, I would stand no chance against a man like him.

"Just answer me," I said. "Are you D.?"

Instead of answering, he lifted the hand that was missing fingers and, with what ones remained, curled them repeatedly as if to signal something. I did not understand this gesture and told him as much.

"Money," he said, hand still outstretched.

"What?"

"If you want answers," he said. "They're gonna cost you."

I reached into my pocket and removed my wallet. Inside it were three twenty dollar bills. I looked up and noticed that he saw them and, not caring to hide it, he smiled. I plucked one out and placed it in the large center of his palm. He rubbed the bill between his fingers before sliding it into his pocket.

"I've been called a lot of names," he said. "For a season or so, I believe D. might've been one of them."

I looked at him then and could not see what I needed to see. And I knew that it had to be this way. That even if I had had all the light and all the time and all the money in the world, I could never know for sure who I was really talking to.

"Next question," he said and started to say something else before pausing.

A loud boom had startled both of us. We looked up in unison at the night sky. Blue and green streams of light, having already exploded, were now falling slowly towards the earth.

In the months and then the years that followed Corrine's disappearance, people who heard what happened asked me, "Didn't you look for her?" By people, I mostly mean women. When I tell them the places I went and even half of the things I did in order to find her, they regret having asked. Because of the myth that computers make it impossible to disappear, they believe that I am leaving something out of my story.

Except that I am not. Corrine walked out of our house that Friday evening wearing a black silk dress with nothing on underneath. Her red hair, still wet from the shower, was gathered together in a loose bun. She kissed me on the mouth and said, "No more slivers for you, Mister. You're going to have to use your imagination."

I have been trapped there ever since.

The fireworks continued overhead, casting the two of us in a shifting array of colors: red then purple then green then red again then, after a long stretch of our original darkness, the brightest blue yet. We watched this initial run then returned to each other's face.

"Next question," he said and performed the same gesture with the maimed hand.

I put a second bill into it and, just as the first time, he rubbed it between his fingers before depositing it in his pocket.

"Corrine," I said. "After she left me, do you know where she went?"

At this he let out a laugh that seemed to come from the back of a cave, one containing coldness and mockery but somehow also a very real sense of brotherhood.

"Gone's gone," he said. "It doesn't matter where she went. She's not here."

I looked at my last bill and thought about my last question. Though the fireworks had paused for a moment, they started back up in a more rapid series of explosions, one color filling the sky before the last one had faded. This made it difficult to focus, much less to think about my question. The color and the sound and the man, who was still looming over me with his massive size and unreadable face: all of this made it impossible to say what I wanted to say.

What I wanted to say was, "It doesn't matter where she ended up, but what matters is, wherever she ended up, is she happy? Is she healed and whole and moving forward in all the most important ways?" What I really wanted to ask, standing there under the fireworks and calling Corrine's beautiful face into my mind's eye, was, "Did she find her way back home?" But these questions did not come to me then. They came to me later that night as I was driving home.

"You down to your last question," he said and, to save me the trouble, reached into my wallet and removed the bill himself. "Make it count."

I did not make it count. The fireworks stopped, and everything got quiet and dark again, and I looked down at the pavement and barely even thought before letting the words come out of my mouth.

"What were you doing there tonight?" I asked. "Why were you in my neighborhood?"

"Big Zac asked me to help," he said.

"Big Zac?" I said. "Who is Big Zac?"

"Big Zac," he said, as if it were impossible not to know who Big Zac was. "The fireworks guy."

The resolution of this one mystery released in my mind the images of several roadside firework stands, each of which, I now remembered, had a massive sign with "Big Zac's Fireworks" painted in red and yellow. Something in my face must have displayed this sudden recognition because, as soon as I realized it, the man reached out and slapped me on the shoulder.

"Yep," he said and gave my upper arm a hard squeeze. "That Zac."

Then he laughed and turned to leave. I wanted to stop him but had become, once more, an empty box: not a thought in my head, not a word in my mouth. I stood there in the dark like the fool I was and watched him get back into his car, again mumbling something underneath his breath (something, this time, that sounded like "Crazy.").

Then I did the same. I climbed into my car, started the engine, and drove back through the darkness to my home across town.

When I got home that night, my wife asked me where I was. I had already engineered a decent lie, something about running to the store to buy a particular brand of wine that she was her favorite. I was going to claim that I wanted to surprise her, but how, after driving around town looking for a store still open for the holiday, I was forced to come home empty handed. My wife, who is generous to the extent that she believes the best in almost everyone, would have believed this story.

Except that when I looked into her eyes, I could not do it.

"Do you want the truth?" I said.

"Of course," she said.

"It's a very long story," I said. "Are you sure you want to hear it?"

Because she asked for it, I told my wife the very long story. The version I gave her omitted nothing: not Doughnut, not Corrine, not Imogene, not Liam, not Ogre, not D., not a single twisted thing we did in the name of love, and not even the stuff about the doors in fairytales. I told my wife the truth as I knew it and, when I was finished, she looked different than before. Her eyes now shined with a different kind of light.

I asked her if she was okay. She told me that she was. She said that if that was the truth, then she was glad to know it.

"The past is the past," she said and blew me a kiss. "Let's go to bed."

We went to bed, and we fell asleep, and in the morning, when I asked her again, she swore that everything was fine. But my wife is not a teller of stories. That new light in her eyes, which may or may not diminish in time, was a light I would know anywhere. It was the light of agony. For a long time yet, it would shine there, seeming to aim itself directly at my heart.

# FIVE STAGES OF HUNGER

---

*Denial*

"You must be hungry," says my husband.

"I could eat," I reply.

I say this without hesitation, but it is a lie. Which is why I deliver it with a code—a face that says, *I'm lying. Please notice that I'm lying.*

The code is designed to lead him to the truth. The truth is I have not been hungry in months. The truth is, after my mother died, food became another tasteless, colorless thing that I could suddenly do without.

Someone told me this would happen and that, in time, the desire to eat would return. But my mother died almost six months ago and everything good still tastes like nothing.

"I'm in the mood for steak," my husband says.

"I could do steak," I lie again and resupply the code by adjusting my eyes to say, *Please, Honey. I. Am. Lying.*

"Perfect," he says. "Let's try that place on Second Avenue."

It is not his fault that he thinks of steaks when I'd rather him think of codes. My husband wasn't raised to think in terms of codes. He is a good man, born in the Midwest and literal as a bucket of snow. He says what he feels and expects others to do the same, Meanwhile I am a Southerner and therefore ruined by ambiguity.

There is also this: everyone he loves is still alive.

Why the code at all? Why not simply speak to my husband like an adult? Other than grief itself, which has made me starved for things I should not want, I have no valid reason.

"Second Avenue," I say and grab my purse off the counter. "Sounds like a plan."

While he is putting on his boots, I stare a hole into his large, reliable shoulders. Something about the size of his back makes me seethe. His head, which is brown and still wet from the shower, takes on the appearance of a football and I nurse the fantasy of kicking it off his thick neck. I would hate this man if I did not love him.

I would hate him if he wasn't so perfect. But he is. He was perfect before my mom got sick, he was perfect when her cancer got worse, and he was perfect at the end, when the pain was so bad that she begged for it to be over, and when I wanted what she wanted, except that I didn't because I still wanted her with me in this world. And now that she's gone, he is perfect still—encouraging me when I can't get out of bed, feeding me when I don't feel like eating, and keeping me in forward motion through a darkness that appears to have no end.

"We will get past this," he says to me, almost daily. "One day at a time, we will move forward."

Why anyone would hate a man like this, I cannot say. But I do. And I hate him most when he forces me to eat. My husband is always forcing me to eat.

As soon as we leave our apartment, he puts his arm around me. I can smell his cologne and, beneath that, the pine-scented soap he has used since we first met. We walk together down Second Avenue and when the restaurant is in view, he leans down and whispers in my ear, "I'm excited."

"Me too," I say.

"Perfect night for steak," he says.

"It is," I say. "It really is."

I have given up on code for the night. I do it his way—I move forward one step at a time.

When we get to the restaurant, we do what we have done thousands of times since we got married eight years earlier. We eat and we drink. One of us asks a question and the other one answers. And when, towards the end of the meal, he asks why I hardly touched my food, I lie without even thinking about it.

"I ate something earlier," I say. "It was a big bowl of cereal."

He laughs and says something about how great it is to have leftovers. And as he laughs, I watch his teeth. They are large and white and neatly arranged in rows. Anyone would be lucky to be married to such teeth, but tonight I do not feel lucky. Tonight his teeth remind me of perfect little tombstones. I want to use the butt end of my steak knife and see how many I can break. I want to scream my mother's name to a roomful of strangers.

My husband reaches across the table and takes my hand in his.

"Let's go home," he says.

"Okay," I say.

We go home and deposit the leftovers in the refrigerator. My husband waits until we are in bed and the lights are off before he touches me. Like food, sex has lost whatever colors it once had. It is a gray and hollow thing, but like eating, it is not hard to lie and to let one moment slip into the next. I let him touch me however he wants. I touch him back in ways that I once meant. In this way, we make love. Then we move to our separate sides of the bed and try to fall asleep.

The last image that comes into my mind before I sleep overtakes me is, strangely, a large red bowl of Rice Crispies cereal. The tiny golden puffs are floating on the whitest milk I've ever seen and I can tell that someone has dipped a spoon into sugar and sprinkled the sugar across the cereal. I almost manage to fall asleep before the sobbing starts.

"Are you okay?" my husband asks.

"I'm fine," I say, choking down the tears.

Rice Crispies—my mother's favorite.

*Anger*

It's dinner time again, several nights later, and my husband says to me, "How do you feel about Italian?"

I consider leaving more code. Code which, upon decipherment, would tell him that I feel nothing about Italian because I feel nothing about everything, especially food. Code which would illuminate for him the reality of my appetite. That I wake up not hungry, that I go to work not hungry, and that in the evenings when he wants to talk about dinner I am not hungry in my compliance.

I am sympathetic with respect to his efforts. I know he has noticed the weight I've lost—twenty, possibly thirty pounds. I know this scares him and I suspect that this is why he works so hard to ensure I eat.

But at the moment, I am tired of being sympathetic. I am tired of the deception and tired of the compliance and tired of scattering code like some kind of breadcrumb trail for him to follow back to the truth. I decide to just tell him the truth.

"I'm not eating anything," I say. "And don't try to force me."

"Did you already eat?" he says and looks confused, a bright-eyed student struggling to solve a tricky equation.

"No," I say and feel my anger tingling in my nail beds. "And I'm not going to."

The tone I use and the face I make is not a code. It is a neon sign composed of two-foot letters, which flash like a cop car and loop in script to spell "LEAVE ME THE FUCK ALONE." Or, better yet, simply "LEAVE ME."

"You have to eat," he says and tries to come close to me.

"No," I say and move away.

"It's not healthy."

"I don't care."

"Part of moving forward is—"

"Stop talking."

"I'm trying to help," he says. "Tell me what I can do to help you."

I answer this question as honestly as I possibly can.

"You can leave me alone," I say.

"Okay," he says and backs away.

Shockingly, my husband honors both requests. He puts on his boots, tells me that he loves me, and leaves the apartment without another word. He stays gone for just over an hour and when he returns he has food for me.

"It's eggplant parmesan," he says through the door to our bedroom, which I have closed and locked. "I'll leave it in the refrigerator."

I say nothing in response. And because I want one more locked door between us, I go into the bathroom. I take a long hot shower in which I don't wash but instead just stand there and let the scalding threads slide down my neck and back.

When I emerge, I stand naked in front of the half-fogged mirror and look at myself. What I see is not good. It is much more than twenty pounds that I have lost. Though the steam softens the blow, I see the sharpened bones in my shoulders. My arms are wasted down to sticks. There are shadows gathering where they shouldn't—in my cheeks and around my hips. What I see is a skeleton.

"Eat," I say to the skeleton, looking directly into its sunken eyes. "You want to live, don't you?"

But to this, the skeleton says nothing. It just stares back, all pale skin and sad veins and poking bones.

Eventually the anger recedes. My husband keeps a bottle of gin in his closet. I drink a third of it and the anger recedes even further. When finally I'm more numb than fractious, I leave our bedroom and join my husband on the couch. I apologize for losing my temper. He brings me the takeout container and I shove bites of eggplant parmesan into my mouth. I tell my teeth to move. They comply.

"It's good, isn't it?" he says.

"It is," I reply.

"You know I'm just looking out for you, right?" he says.

"I do," I reply.

"And you know we're going to get through this, right?"

"I do."

"One day at a time," he says and kisses me directly atop my skeleton cheek.

*Bargaining*

Weeks go by. Or maybe it's months. Another thing they never told me about grief is what it does to time. Grief turns time into a splintered, swerving mess. I have good days and I have bad ones. My husband has only good ones. He persists in his perfect array of duties—listening and encouraging and loving and forgiving and, each night at exactly six-o'clock, ensuring I receive bodily nourishment. Because of his persistence, I gain ten pounds. My husband is pleased but reminds me that I need to gain even more.

"Hey," I tell him. "Ten pounds is a small watermelon."

He laughs and congratulates me on gaining a small watermelon.

"The bottom line," he says. "Is that you're looking better every day."

My husband says this so often that I am beginning to think he means "You're *getting* better every day." He has never admitted this conflation, but he doesn't need to. I know how he thinks about progress. That the best kind of progress is progress that's visible: points on a scoreboard; pounds on a scale. A Midwestern literalist, he understands things best when he can see them.

What he cannot see, and what I have not told him, is

that food, like most things, still seems empty to me. I don't desire food anymore than I desire to get out of bed or shower or go to work. He aims to remedy this by making the foods I used to love. Except that even the foods I used to love—pineapple pizza and chocolate chip pancakes and grilled cheese sandwiches served with tomato basil soup—have all lost their power to move me.

"I could go for Mexican," he says one night, right on cue, as the clock on the microwave hits six o'clock. "Fish tacos. Chips and salsa. Maybe one of those margaritas you love with the little umbrella?"

The word "umbrella" makes me think of rain, which makes me think of my mother's funeral, which makes me think of all those black umbrellas, which made it hard to tell who was who, and which also made it so I could barely hear the priest above the slap of rain on plastic. When my husband calls my name, I am no longer thinking of umbrellas. I am trying to remember whether it was orchids or chrysanthemums that were arranged by my mother's casket.

"Honey?" he says and actually claps his hands. "How does Mexican sound to you?"

Instead of answering him, I pray. To God, to the Universe, to whomever or whatever is listening, I pray, *Let my hunger come back. Let me move forward and want the things I'm supposed to want. If you do this, I'm yours.*

"Honey?" says my husband. "Are you okay?"

"What's that?" I say, still waiting for God's response.

Praying reminds me of my father, who spent so much time kneeling down beside my mother's hospital bed that his knees and shins became covered with bruises. I wonder what he tried to bargain in return for my mother's life. I wonder how he felt to know that, whatever he offered wasn't good enough.

"Are you sure you're okay?" my husband says to me.

"Mexican sounds fine," I say and, as he bends down to put on his boots, I realize something about my husband—that though he likely prays for many things, he has never prayed for a life.

*Depression*

"Whatever" is what I say to my husband when tells me that he intends to cook lasagna for dinner. Much time has passed and I have gotten worse, not better. I am done with codes and confrontations. I have resorted to inebriated growls.

Something about "Whatever" concerns him. Maybe it's the frequency with which I now use it, the way it has replaced "Yes" and "No" and even "I don't know." Or maybe he thinks it's emblematic of other recent changes—my getting fired for too many absences; my moving from drinking wine at night to drinking bourbon whenever I feel like it; my overeating and undershowering, which has effectively transported me from skeleton to troll. Maybe, for him, "Whatever" is the word that captures just how bad things have become.

Because the moment I say "Whatever" to his plan for lasagna, he comes out of the kitchen and confronts me.

"How drunk are you?" he says.

"Not drunk enough," I say and want nothing more than to get this over with.

He grows silent at this. He bites his bottom lip in the way he does before saying something he is afraid to say.

"I think," he starts. "That it's time you see someone. A professional, I mean."

For this, I summon something other than "Whatever." For this, I look him dead in the eyes and say, "No."

"It's almost been a year," he says.

"No," I say.

"I've been asking around," he says. "I found someone who I think would be really great for you. She's been a grief counselor for—"

"I said no. End of discussion."

This is where I get up from the couch and walk away, not fast and violent as in the angry days, but stumbly and slow enough to tell him what, in many ways, he already knows—that I could not possibly care less about whatever he has to say. He yells at my back as I cross the room.

"What makes you think you get to end the discussion?"

"Because," I say, not bothering to turn around. "I don't want to talk to a professional and I definitely don't want to talk to you."

"Well," he shouts. "You better start wanting to talk."

I have reached the door to our bedroom and intend to enter, lock it behind me, and pass out on the bed. And yet, I am intrigued by his last remark. That is, I am intrigued by the way he said it—as if it were a threat.

Still in the doorway, I turn to face him.

"What does that mean?" I say.

"It means you can't go on like this."

"And what if I do?" I say. "What if I never get better? What then? You'll leave?"

"Is that what you want?" he says. "You want me to leave?"

I take longer than I should to answer this question, in which time he wrings his large hands like some small and worried child. Also, though I cannot be sure, from where I am standing it looks like his eyes are covered with the film of new tears. I watch him for a moment. I watch his little boy eyes, waiting to see if anything comes out. When it doesn't, and when I feel so tired that I could fall asleep right there in the doorway, I stand there and open my mouth. That's all it takes for the old refrain to follow.

"Whatever," I say before closing the door.

I use the bathroom before going to bed and only briefly do I look in the mirror on my way out. The troll that lives there is worse than the skeleton. I hate its sad and puffy face. I hate its greasy hair and bloodshot eyes. I hate the defeated slump that never leaves its shoulders. So I say the most hurtful thing I can before turning off the lights and climbing into bed.

"If mom saw you like this," I say to the troll. "She would be so disappointed."

*Acceptance*

"Wake up," says my husband.

I do and see that morning has flooded our bedroom. I feel tired and hungover and hopeless, as I do most mornings these days. And yet, there is something about this light. There is something about the way my husband walks through it and sits down on the bed. I do not feel hope, per se, but some minor sense of possibility.

"Come on," he says and rubs my back. "I made us breakfast."

"Is there coffee?" I say.

"Yes," he says. "Strong coffee."

I sit up and compose my thoughts. I remember last night, or enough of it to know that I feel ashamed of my behavior.

"I didn't expect you to be here," I admit. "I thought you'd be gone."

"I live here," he says. "Remember?"

He takes my hand in his and squeezes it. Then he brings it to his mouth and kisses me on the knuckles. I feel his teeth against my skin and don't, at this moment, completely want to break them. In fact, in this moment, I feel some level of ownership is called for.

"I'm sorry about last night," I say.

"It's okay," he says.

"No it's not," I say. "None of it is. I've been horrible lately."

"It's okay," he says.

"I don't really want you to leave."

"Good," he says. "Because I'm not. Now get out of bed and come to the table before everything gets cold."

I join my husband at the table, where there is scrambled eggs and buttered toast, fresh coffee and orange juice. We sit down together and he fixes me a plate. For the first time in months, today feels like it might be a good day. And yet, before it can be a good day, there is something I have to tell him, something I only now am able to put into words.

"I need you to do something for me," I say. "Actually, I need you to *stop* doing something for me."

"Okay," he says. "What is it?"

"Stop saying that I'm going to get through this."

"But you will. It'll take time, but you're going to—"

"No," I say. "I don't want to get through this."

Quicker than I knew they could, tears pour out of my eyes and grief folds me over the table. I weep and I tremble and I scream. My husband reaches over and puts his hand on my back. When I finally I sit up again, I use my napkin to blow my nose.

"She was my mom," I say, still crying. "She still is my mom. And I don't want to move past her. I want to stay with her for as long as I can."

He thinks about this for a long time, so long that I collect myself and reach out for his hand.

"Okay," he says. "But let me ask you something."

"What?"

"If you don't want to move forward," he says. "What do you want to do?"

There are many things I want to tell him in this moment. How I need him to stop being so perfect. How some nights I need him to just say nothing and hold me while we watch bad television. How other nights I need him to tell me every story he has about my mom, no matter how small or silly he believes it to be. How I love him more than anyone on the planet and how even though I am not moving past my mother's death, I want to not move past it with him.

I want to say all of this, but I don't say any of it. Instead, I pick up a piece of toast and spread blackberry jam across it.

I cut it into two triangles and lift one to my mouth. I take a small bite out of the corner and, instead of chewing it, I hold the bite in my mouth for as long as I can, so long the butter that has mixed with the blackberry jam drips off the bread and onto my tongue.

My mouth is full of sweetness when I answer my husband's question. I say to him, "How about we try eating?"

# A BRIEF QUESTIONNAIRE FOR THE CREATURE THAT BECAME THE FUR THAT BECAME THE COAT THAT MY WIFE RECEIVED FROM HER RICH FRIEND THEN WORE OBSESSIVELY ALL WINTER

I.

What (in life) were you? Your fur is white, and I assume from such whiteness that, pre-conversion, you were some fetching breed of arctic creature. But that's the kind of guess rendered useless by its own generality, since I know nothing about the Arctic, nor do I know which of its creatures are hunted for their fur, nor for that matter do I know when it became normal to wear body parts for fashion rather than survival. The internet said you could have been a fox, a rabbit, a mink, a raccoon dog, a muskrat, a beaver, a stoat, an otter, a seal, a cat, a dog, a coyote, a wolf, a chinchilla, or a common brushtail possum, so I need you to ground me in the specifics of your existence. I am trying to make a connection here.

II.

Let's go back (if it's not too painful) to the time before you became the fur that became the coat that my wife received from her rich friend then wore obsessively all winter. Let's go back (if it's okay with you) to your final moments as you. Forgive my morbidity, but did you see your killer? Was there a chase involved? Were your children bearing witness? This is my philosophy and maybe you share it: if you can't let me be, don't kill me in front of my family. If your murderers did not extend to you this courtesy, shame on them. I will pray now, as I'm sure you did, that the lucre generated by your death installs a curse upon everyone involved. Lord, may any man who smiled to see this creature die one day see his own death coming slow as a rider in the distance. May there be fear and smallness and shame.

## III.

I don't want to make you uncomfortable, but what, if anything, would you say to your killers? Let's pretend you could come back for one day. What would have the best chance at converting them from murderous assholes to large-hearted saints? (Is it justice or grace that rearranges a heart? I can never tell.) What if I could get you a year? Would that make a difference? I am not optimistic where the repentance of killers is concerned. Are you? I think greed is the thickest ice of all the ices around our consciences. If I could secure it, would you want another lifetime to come back and try to break that ice, or would you rather I just let you keep sleeping? It's your call. Either way, no judgment.

## IV.

Speaking of judgment, what do you know about this rich woman who gave you (or what is left of you) to my wife? The reason I ask is this: the other day I walked in on my wife as she was looking at herself in the mirror. She was wearing you. She was wearing nothing but you, her long brown legs cast out in front of her, her elegant neck thrown back to catch the light of the overhead bulb. I should've found this sexy. I should've held her and said something about how lovely she looked. But I couldn't. Because when I looked at her, all I saw was the rich woman. The rich woman's legs, the rich woman's neck, and (you must believe me when I tell you this) the lush, curling self-confidence of the rich woman's smile. My wife, as if emulating her friend, had become a stranger to me. You know a thing or two about transference, so tell me this: should I be concerned here?

V.

Final question, I promise: if your body is here with us, where are you? And what of the distance between the place where you are and the place where we are, the place where (in case you don't know) we're still killing your kind for the sake of our fashion? Is that distance so great that the transactions of earth become tolerable, even humorous, in their microscopic cruelties? Or is it the other way? Are you closer now than ever before? So close that all the lines we used to abide by have become useless and blurred, killers now saints, saints now wolves, the poor rich and the rich poor, all one, ice broken and hearts recovered, all one, your body now my body, the two of us all one, one, one. Answer me this: is that tired dream of solidarity any less laughable in the place where you are?

# THE DEVIL IS BEATING HIS WIFE

Inevitable that it started on a porch, it being Clemson and the '80s and the lush red middle of a Carolina autumn. And though it was the porch of our own house, we should not have been there, neither Lazarus nor I. Where we should have been was a half-mile into campus, in a sad little room with walls the color of regurgitated oatmeal, where a Southern Lit professor was waiting to tell us about a Faulkner novel neither of us had bothered buying. The class was called "The Old South" and, since attending its opener, Laz and I had skipped all subsequent gatherings. The sweet old guy's mythology, while riveting, lacked traction. We could not suffer it.

It was this kind of indifference that made graduation in the spring increasingly unlikely. But, on the bright side, it was because we forgot "The Old South" that we were positioned on the porch just after sunrise to hear the screen door slam and see Joe, our longtime roommate, stumble out of the house looking stuck somewhere between a nightmare and a punchline. Joe was shirtless and had used duct tape to wrap his hands and knees in strips of tire. He made for an ambiguous beast, pitiful but not yet robbed of pride.

"Behold," said Laz, lit Philly fixed in the corner of his smirk. "Our resident deep-fried Romeo."

"Stay put!" croaked Joe and without looking at either of

us lowered himself into the stance of a dog and crawled off the porch.

Like two men who've wandered into the same dream, Laz and I stood up and watched Joe use his jimmy-rigged paws to advance across the yard and onto the dirty pavement of Boudreaux boulevard.

"It's Tuesday," observed Laz. "Doesn't he have his Milton class at nine?"

I said nothing. For one, like Laz, I knew that whatever this was had something to do with Katie, Joe's longtime girl. On a deeper level, though, recent events had inclined me to silence. I'd seen a striped tabby stray named Penny appear in our window three days after we found her dead in the street and buried her. I'd seen a woman with bone-white hair run naked down the block at dawn crying, "Reset! Reset! Reset!" And, two nights ago, I'd seen a black Cadillac, no driver, circle our street while a blood moon hung in the night sky like an iced plum.

It's true I came to Clemson a privileged hick with answers for everything, but the wild and difficult poetry of our senior year had shut me up.

"College boys and their college girls," said Laz, waving his long finger in my face and tisking out a tongue-cadence like some disapproving parent. "Are y'all not yet weary of this ancient cycle?"

After several moments of us just standing there, and Joe scrambling down Boudreaux, and the sweetness of our porch conspiring with the crunchy red leaves scattered across the lawn as if all was still lovely and ordained, I maintained my vow of silence but took off after Joe, catching him just before he turned left on Sarkey. Laz slapped his thighs and said, "By the hand of a God I no longer believe in, I swear it's time for something new!" With fierce reluctance, he followed.

"Hold up," I said, crouching in front of Joe and grabbing him by his shoulders.

Already sweat had bubbled in little pods across Joe's back.

His face was cough-syrup purple and licked with dust. I didn't like what I was seeing: a broken man on a bad quest, all nightmare and no punchline, once you got up close. Glass half full, however, his paws were holding up just fine.

"Move!" Joe grunted, writhing in all directions against my grip.

"Speak," I replied. "Tell me what's going on here."

"I'll tell you what's going on," said Laz, the only one not breathing hard. "He's lost his girl and this is him winning her back. Joe, old buddy, have you considered a phone call? I bet Katie would appreciate that. Or how about a handwritten letter with a nice line from Yeats?"

I had dug my hands into Joe's shoulders and sprawled out so as to smother him with my full weight. He wasn't going anywhere but had yet to come around an acceptance of that reality.

"Move!" he screamed and continued pressing into me.

Laz lit a new cigar and said, "If self-flagellation is what you're after, I have a Civil War documentary back at the house. We can watch it together and I'll remind you what thieving ugly shits your people have been these last three centuries."

Joe didn't answer. He persisted. The sharp scratching on pavement, the unified throb of so many sunlit muscles: you knew it was noble even as you knew it was pointless. All I had to do was lean on him. And all Laz could do was watch my leaning until, after mustering one final torque, Joe's arms buckled and he collapsed.

"Enough," I said.

"That's right. Enough," Laz echoed. "Come home and I'll buy you a box of that beer you like."

Twice Joe tried to raise himself up. Both times I pinned him back to the ground. Following that he thrashed his head from side to side, ramming at empty air until his skull cracked against the pavement. A gash opened up above his left eye and a red rope descended through sweat and dust and sunlight. Joe used his forearm to wipe it and left a crimson smear across his forehead like some antique painted warrior.

"This is pointless," I said. "What's your goal here?"

"What's yours?" growled Joe.

Laz laughed and, approaching us, patted Joe between the shoulder blades. I momentarily relaxed my grip. Laz said, "Joe, you ever read Camus's thing on Sisyphus? How when you look at him pushing that boulder, you have to imagine—"

On "imagine," Joe exploded off the pavement and drove his head into the slack center of my gut. Down I went. Down Laz went too, though he hadn't even been touched. By the time we found our feet, Joe was gone, clear around the corner for Sarkey.

"Come on!" I said, motioning Laz back to the house. "Plan B."

"Plan B?" Laz mocked.

Plan B was this: we'd use the moped to shoot ahead of Joe and set up at what I called "checkpoints." Plan B was walking with a man you could not stop. Sometime between getting knocked on my ass and returning to our house, I had completed the rough calculations.

"Our boy's moving at 2 miles an hour," I said. "If it's 6 miles to Katie's place, we'll set up once at Freedie's. Again at The Recovery Room. And a final time at Old Son's. That's three legs to home."

I watched Laz run the logistics in his head. Truth is, it worked out, right down to the three bars breaking Joe's journey into three equal stretches.

"That's the dumbest thing I've ever heard," Laz said. "I want nothing to do with this scheme. I'd rather sit on this porch and hit both of my pinky toes with a claw hammer."

But when I revved the moped and started out of the driveway, Laz hopped on.

"For the record," Laz said, as we sped down Boudreaux. "I'd rather be reading Faulkner."

My math was off. We drank at Freedie's for two hours with no sign of Joe. Which was fine by us. Killing time with talk and booze was exactly what we'd be doing back at Boudreaux.

"Tell me what I'm missing about your kind," said Laz, who already had a steady buzz going. "Tell me a single thing to redeem this pitiful endeavor."

I did not know and would not ask what Laz meant by my "kind." There was no point. It could've meant region, since both Joe and I were from Carolina whereas Laz hailed from somewhere in Alabama. It could've referred to sexuality, since both Joe and I would gladly drink the bathwater of the women we loved and Laz was, by his own admission, asexual. But likely what it meant was all three of those distinctions and ten more we didn't even know existed. Because that was Laz's gift--exiling himself from whatever categories the too-tidy South could conjure up.

"Okay," I said. "Love."

"Love?" Laz said and was smirking as if speaking with a child who received a C-minus in comprehension. "And when Katie opens her door and looks down on his sorry ass, what will love get him?"

"If it works, she'll think he's sorry. If it really works, she'll take him back."

This drew a laugh from Laz. He killed his vodka-tonic in one large gulp and readjusted his little black baron fedora. It's worth noting that Laz extended his pilgrim status straight into the aesthetical realm. He wore black, regardless of the occasion. Black shirt, black jeans, black boots, and that fedora, which sat askew on his head like a thing poached from John Dillinger's dumpster. His attire, so dark and loose and strange, made it impossible to tell, even close up, if he was male or female, heavy metal or homeless. To further dislodge him from what he often called "the teeming mass of humanity," Laz routinely shaved every inch of his body, including his scalp and his eyebrows. No one, not even Joe and I, who had roomed with Laz since freshman year, knew what to make of him, other than the plain fact that he was as alone as any one person could be, struck from the map of all conceivable categories, and therefore able to to critique our kind or any other kind with relative impunity.

"I know a bit about love," Laz said.

"Is that right?"

"My mother was Baptist," he said. "Have I ever told you that?"

He had not and I admitted as much. I finished the drink in front me and realized that I, too, was nursing a nice fog.

"She was," Laz continued. "A very serious Baptist, actually. And do you know what my father was?"

"What?"

"A very serious drinker," he said and flagged down the bartender for another vodka-tonic. When his drink arrived, he continued: "And when my old man had been drinking, he did not exercise what you would call good judgement. After hitting the bars, he would come home, not mean or abusive, but just very late and very drunk. And do you know what my mother would do when he came home?"

"What?"

"She would bolt the door shut and make my father enter the house through the doggy door."

"You're kidding."

"I'm not," Laz said. "And my father, not a small man, would do it. It became a kind of ritual for them. Her standing there in the hall like some kind of bronze statue of a martyr. And him grunting loud enough to wake half the neighborhood and busting half the muscles in his back squeezing through that door."

"That's wild," I said and tried to envision my own father doing such a thing. I could not.

"But get this," Laz replied. "I remember this one time when it happened, and I got out of bed, and I snuck over to the top of the stairs where I could watch. And my father, who was that night especially sloshed, could only make it halfway through the doggy door. He had worked his head, shoulders, and chest through, but his gut had gotten caught and he was too drunk and too tired to yank it all the way through."

"So what did he do?"

"He looked up at my mom and said, 'Why do you do this to me, Fran? Does it make you hot to see me hurt like this?' And from the top of the stairs I watched my mother do a strange thing. I watched her walk over to where he was stuck, slip out of her panties, lift her nightgown over her hips, and lower her bare bottom directly onto his face. And I watched as my old man smiled and used to his tongue to—"

"Ugh," I muttered. "No more. Why tell me this?"

"Because," Laz said. "If that's love, you can keep it. I don't believe in it. I'm ready for something new."

"No disrespect to your parents, Laz, but this is different. Joe loves Katie. If this is his way of showing it, I'm in no position to judge."

"Love," Laz said, ridding his mouth of the word like it was an especially lowly form of fungus.

"Yes," I said. "Love. It's a thing. You should try it sometime."

"Love," Laz continued. "Is like the elephant and the blind men. Surely you, an English major and a runaway Presbyterian, are familiar with that parable?"

"No," I admitted. "I'm not."

"An elephant comes to town," Laz said. "Three men, all blind since birth, approach the great beast. One grabs it by the ear and says to his friends, 'I know now what an elephant is! It is soft and floppy like a blanket.' When the second blind man hears this, he becomes upset. You see, the second blind man is holding the elephant by its leg. 'You are a liar!' he screams. 'I am touching the elephant now and it is big and sturdy like a tree.' The first and second blind man begin to fight and become so engrossed in their argument that they cannot hear the third blind man, who is holding the elephant by his tail and swearing by heaven and earth that elephants are thin, stick-like creatures. Now, Colonel Mustard, do you have ears to hear what I'm saying or not?"

"I get it," I said. "It's a nice parable."

"And that's a nice blind man," Laz replied and pointed out of the bar's window and down towards the street. It was Joe.

Joe refused to come in. Committed to his new form, he refused to even sit up while we spoke to him. The best we got was a nod or shake.

"You ready to go home and get that beer?" I said.

Shake.

"You ready to tell us what this is all about?"

Shake.

"Well, you look like shit," said Laz. "At least let us get you some water."

Joe, meeting our eyes for what might have been the first time that day, wiped the sweat from his eyes and nodded.

Laz ducked into the pharmacy and returned with a bottle of water, a blue plastic bowl, and a tube of sunscreen. After Laz had set the bowl on the pavement and filled it with water, Joe plunged his face into it and attacked the liquid with a desperate series of gulps. While Laz used a napkin to clean the cut above his eye, I opened the sunscreen and applied it generously to Joe's back and arms and calves, all of which were already darkening with the pink beginning of a bad burn.

When Joe had finished drinking and looked apt to leave, I knelt beside him and said, "If you're heading to Katie's, wouldn't a moped get you there a little quicker?"

"It would," Joe said, using his teeth to adjust the tire strapped to his left hand. "But it would also miss the point."

Sensing that we'd lose him at any moment, I said, "But what's the point, Joe?"

"If I make to Katie's place, you'll see," he said.

Then he was gone. We lingered for a while to watch him go. People on the sidewalk jumped back as he crawled past.

A little girl dropped her lollipop and cried. Then a fat, hateful-looking white man with a patchy beard and a camouflage hat pulled up in a truck began yelling something at Joe. From the back of this angry chub's vehicle waved the largest Confederate flag I'd ever seen in my life. The flag dwarfed the truck. Whatever this man was yelling, Joe wasn't responding. And, failing to get his desired response, Flag Boy chucked a bottle of dip-spit at Joe's head. The bottle struck him squarely, spilling its brown slime across Joe's neck and back. Flag Boy then slapped his hand on the side of his truck and laughed as if the funniest joke in the world had just been made just for him. Then he threw something else, something that made a sharp, metallic clank when it hit the pavement in front of Joe's face. Sounded like a wrench.

"'Old South' my ass," I said. "Let's drag that racist asshole out of his truck and kick his teeth in."

"That," Laz said. "Would miss the point."

We left Joe there and took back roads to The Recovery Room.

As at Freedie's, we ordered drinks at The Recovery Room and resumed our talk. We killed a good half hour discussing strategies for bullshitting our way through our class. Laz happened to know a guy who knew his Faulkner. I happened to know our old professor's favorite bourbon. Failure did not concern us. Following that, we sat for a while and said nothing, just watched the television above the bar, which was showing one of those daytime talk shows where couples who hate each other publicly receive the results of paternity tests. We watched a young man with shitty teeth and neck tattoos get confirmation that he was not the father of the child in question. The mother wept into her own arms. The man jumped up and down, pumping his fists in celebration, as if he had just won the lottery.

"I'm free!" the man screamed and extended not one but two stiff middle fingers at the weeping woman, his non-wife, non-mother-of-his-child. "From here on out, I don't want to hear shit about that baby!"

"Well," said Laz. "If that's not emblematic of our present state of affairs, I don't what is."

I laughed and, sensing the talk was about to circle back to Joe, made up my mind to ask a question I'd been sitting on ever since I met Lazarus. I said, "Hey, Laz, what are you going to do after graduation?"

Laz glared at me for asking this. It was the kind of look you gave someone for farting in a hot car.

"Why you asking?" he said.

"Because I'm genuinely curious," I said. "I always have been."

Laz nodded, apparently accepting this as a valid motivation. Then he smiled widely and said, "I think I'll hang myself from the Centennial Oak. Possibly with a quote from Baldwin stapled to my chest."

"Stop," I said. "Be serious. What are your plans?"

"Who knows?" he said and shrugged. "Maybe I'll join the winos down in Easley. Failing that, I could always teach high school English. What about you?"

"I don't know," I said because, for me, there was nothing on earth more true.

"Think you'll marry that girl you're always bringing back to the house? The rich white one with the nice teeth and the fat can?"

I didn't deign to answer this. Laz knew Madison's name, just as he knew that I had worked doubles at Nick's Tavern last summer to save up for an engagement ring. Laz being Laz, he probably even knew that the ring was sitting in my sock drawer, just waiting around, like Madison herself, for me to make up my mind.

"Let me ask you something," I said, figuring it was as good a time as ever to fire off one more thing I'd always been curious about.

"Shoot," said Laz.

"You really don't believe in love?"

"Nope."

"And you plan to spend your entire life alone?"

"That's right."

"What happened to you?" I said. "Have you always been this way?"

"I loved someone once," said Laz. "His name was Homer."

"Well," I said. "Tell me about Homer."

"He was an old thirty-buck mutt we rescued," said Laz. "I must have been about seven or eight years old when we got him. And I took old Homer everywhere with me. Even took him in bed until Mama found ticks in the sheets and exiled Homer to our sorry excuse for a backyard."

"What else?" I said. "Keep going."

Such vulnerability from Laz was rare. In our years of living together, he'd dropped his guard less than a dozen times. With respect to information on his past, I would push him as far as he would allow me to.

"Let's see," Laz said and could not hide his smile. "Homer had a limp. He had it when we got him. Never knew why. Probably his previous owner was some mouthbreather who kicked him around for fun. He'd try his best to run with you but he never could keep up. You'd look over your shoulder and see him hoofing it like the devil was on his heels."

Something was changing in Laz's face and in his voice. I did not like where things were heading but lacked the heart to stop him.

Laz continued: "I was coming home one night. I'd been out nightswimming. Homer was right behind me. At least I thought he was. And I had almost made it my house when I heard a sound too awful to tell. I thought someone had fired a gun. It was that loud. When I turned around, I saw this car speeding off. There's a stop sign at the end of our street and they blew right through it. Just a pair of tail lights fading off into the night."

Laz was holding the bar with both hands and wincing,

like a fighter squinting into an impending blow. And yet, he looked as if he was going to continue with the story, which I did not want him to do.

"That's enough," I said. "I understand."

"Then I saw Homer," he said. "He was smeared across the street. The entire back half of his body had been crushed and more blood than I'd ever seen was spreading like rain across the pavement."

"Okay," I repeated. "Enough."

"Hold on, though, because here's the point. Homer kept on coming. He was dead and didn't even know it, but his eyes were locked on me and his front legs were scrambling like there was still a chance. And I'll never forget that. Homer, smeared across the street, but right up to the end fighting his way back home."

"Damn, Laz."

"I know."

I was going to say something dumb and insensitive, something like "I can see why you don't believe in shit. If I had your past, I wouldn't believe in shit, either." But I never got the chance. A sound was coming from outside, the swelling volume of which pulled us from our conversation. It was the sound of many feet moving at once and a flood of unfamiliar voices all swirling together. We looked outside and saw Joe. He was no longer alone.

The situation outside was absurd. In addition to the two dozen followers who had formed in a loose ring around Joe, there were three news crews, a street-corner preacher, and some girl with a nose-ring holding up a hand-painted sign that read 'MEAT IS MURDER!' The reporters were talking into their cameras, periodically motioning back at Joe. The street preacher was distributing small blue pamphlets to anyone who'd have them, while the girl with the sign was thrashing around behind the reporters, screaming about an upcoming bill. I also noticed Flag Boy riding high in his truck. He'd been joined by a couple of equally large and angry-looking white dudes, all of whom were having a good laugh over Joe's pain.

Our first minute with Joe was spent stripping him of the various accessories he'd accumulated since our last checkpoint. Two flags, one Clemson and the other Palmetto, had been draped over his neck. His back was plastered with stickers, some for indie bands and some for local politicians. All four pockets of his jeans were stuffed full with takeout menus and business cards.

"You've developed quite a following," I said, peeling a "Bird Dog's BBQ" sticker off Joe's ribcage.

As if he had not noticed until that very moment, Joe glanced at the crowd and shrugged.

"How are you holding up?" I asked.

Nod.

"Let's get some food in you before this next leg," I said. "How's that sound?"

Shake.

"Then at least drink some water," I said, filling the blue bowl with water and sliding it under Joe's face.

Joe drank. Meanwhile, one of the reporters approached us. She was short, blonde, and, a couple years past pretty, had buried her smiling face beneath about a quarter-pound of make-up.

"Excuse me, gentlemen," she said, arranging herself beside us while still smiling into the camera. "You seem to be acquainted with this man. Can you speak towards his purpose? Can you tell us why he's doing this?"

"No," I said, swatting her microphone away as if it were a gnat that had forgotten its place.

Entirely unfazed, the blonde continued: "It's been suggested that this is some kind of statement. Is it related to the racial issues in the upcoming election? Is it a symbol of Senator Wilson's refusal to—"

"I said no!" I yelled. "Now get back!"

The rest of the crowd drew back. The blonde, however, remained. "How do you two know 'The Crawler'?" she said. "Can you at least tell us that much?"

"'The Crawler'?" Laz said, looking along with me into the blonde's television-tight eyes.

"Yes," she said. "That's what people are calling him."

Before we could make a decision regarding the most diplomatic way to drive back the blonde and the rest of the clingers, a fight broke out between the girl with the nose-ring and a woman who must have weighed three hundred pounds. The large woman was attempting to rip the sign out of the girl's hands, screaming as she did something about God commanding men to subdue animals. The girl with the nose-ring was landing mean left hooks onto the christian's quivering jowls. Flag Boy, who had a can of beer in his hand, whooped and laid on the horn. When the cameras swung to capture the brawl, we led Joe around the corner and into an alley.

"Halfway home," I said, dabbing at the cut above his eye, which had stopped bleeding but was still glistening in its freshness. "How you feeling?"

"Strong," said Joe and did not resist me prying bits of broken glass and pebbles out of his paws.

"Good," I said. "Your entourage isn't slowing your pace, are they?"

"They won't be around much longer," said Joe, looking up at the sky. "The Devil's about to beat his wife."

We looked up. Sure enough, with the sun shining fat and yellow in the middle of the blue sky, warm drops of rain began splattering the ground around us. Harder than I knew rain could fall, it came from the sky in buckets and drenched everything in sight. The news crews jumped into their vans. The crowd either ducked into The Recovery Room or took off running down the street. We sat there together in the alley and let it soak our faces and hair and bodies. We squinted upwards, in awe of that rare conspiracy between sun and storm.

Eventually, Joe began to move.

"Onward and upward," Laz said flatly and slapped Joe on the ass as he crawled by.

Noticeably slower, Joe moved out of the alley and made his way down Saint Mark's. We settled our tab with The Recovery Room and ran through the rain for the moped. We had revved it and nearly pulled off when a body appeared before us.

"Let me just ask you one question," the face, dripping wet and spitting water.

Laz and I studied the figure. It took us a moment to place him. We did, though, eventually. It was the street preacher, his blue pamphlets a pulpy bouquet stuffed down into a tightly clenched fist.

"What assurance do you have of your future salvation?" he screamed.

"Out of our way!" I said, whipping the moped to the left.

But the preacher jumped with us, grabbing the handlebars and planting his feet.

"You could die tonight, son!" he shouted. "And if you did, do you suppose you'd gain access to the new heaven and the new earth?"

"Fuck your access," Laz replied and I gave the moped gas.

The moped jumped forward. I don't know if the bike struck him or if he flung himself to avoid the collision, but the preacher went down. I do know this: as we sped down the wet road towards Saint Mark's, he was back on his feet and shouting, "Repent! Repent! Repent and believe!"

It was still pouring when we got to Old Son's. Sully, the manager there, gave us each a towel and made us dry off before coming inside. Once we did, we took a booth with a good view of the street and started on the Beam. You could almost see Katie's house from the street outside the bar. She lived in a little yellow house up on the hill.

"Fuck your access and fuck your love," Laz said, once he was several whiskeys in and thoroughly drunk from all the day's drinks. "Love's not real. Throw love in with the other revisionist lies and social constructions. Burn all that shit to cinders. We're in here talking out our asses, and Joe's out there killing himself for a bad joke."

"You're missing the point," I said.

"There's a point now?" Laz said. "What is it?"

"The point is not what's real," I said. "The point is find whatever keeps you from hanging yourself. Find a reason, any reason, to move forward."

"Moving forward," Laz said and winked at me. "Boy, we're crushing that one down here, aren't we? But I've seen how that little view plays itself out.

"Yeah?"

"Yeah," Laz said. "It's like this fool I knew back in high school. He used to put rocks in his shoes then walk around."

"Rocks? Why rocks?"

"Said it was for Jesus."

"Shit," I said. "But why? Why would Jesus want to hurt him?"

"You know, believe it or not, I asked him about that. But the son of a bitch would never give me a straight answer. I must've asked him a hundred times. After a while he just smile at me and, with this weird look in his eyes, say, 'At the center of love is death.'"

"That's deep," I admitted.

"About as deep as a man crawling across the county line for love."

"You're still missing the point."

"Tell me, then, General Pickett," Laz said, smirking. "What is the point?"

"The point is broken people have to believe in something. It doesn't matter what. Love's a better church than money. It's better than the shitshow out there."

Laz let out a series of disapproving tisks. Then he said, "The only thing your kind is in love with is licking their own wounds. That must be a Southern thing. I used to live in Colorado. The men out there eat sushi and climb mountains. You don't see anyone scraping pavement with their gut in the name of love."

"I don't believe that," I replied.

"Believe this," he said and from his pocket pulled two folded pieces of paper and slid them across the table. I opened them. They were letters, one from Katie to Joe and one from Joe to Katie.

"Found those when I was cleaning all those menus out of his pockets," said Laz.

"And?"

"Read them," said Laz.

I slid the letters back to Laz. A look of disappointment, even betrayal, flashed across his face.

"You not going to read them?" he said. "Hell of an English major you are."

"Why? What's the point?"

"We've been wondering this whole time what he did. It's all right there. Read it."

"Did he go somewhere he shouldn't have?"

"He did."

"Did he lie about it?"

"Somewhat."

"Did he swear to Katie, after the fact, that it meant nothing and will never happen again?"

"Basically."

"So what's to read? I get it. Hell, I've lived it."

"Live this," Laz muttered, unfolding the letter and scanning its contents for the line he had in mind.

"'Katie, please believe me,'" Laz read, doing his best impression of Joe's voice. "'Please believe me that nothing in this world could stop me from loving you. I am sorry for what I did, what I still do. I won't always be this way. Please forgive me while I am.'"

Laz paused and looked up. In his normal voice he said, "Those are Joe's words."

"So what?" I said.

"You ready for Katie's response?"

"I don't need to—"

"'I don't believe you,'" Laz continued over me, now high-pitched and imitating Katie. "'I think you are a liar. I think you've lied for so long you no longer know you're doing it. But I'll tell you what, if this is real, why don't you show me how sorry you are?'"

Laz refolded the letter and slid it in his pocket.

"I rest my case," said Laz. "If that's your version of love, then you can keep it. I choose not to believe in it."

"I will keep it," I said.

"Why?"

"Because there's shit else going," I said. "And because if there was something new out there, we would have found it by now."

I watched Laz's face when I said this, expecting some kind of reaction. But Laz was neither looking at me nor listening to me. His gaze, widened and stuffed with something like concern, had cast itself towards the street. I whipped around and saw what was breaking Laz's heart. It broke mine too.

Outside, Flag Boy and three of his friends had circled around Joe. They were spitting beer onto his head and riding him like a horse. They were sticking the bottoms of their boots into his face. Then Joe said something. Whatever it was turned their violence serious. They started kicking Joe for real. I saw one man connect with his ribs. I saw Flag Boy smash him in his teeth. Laz saw this too but seemed to have entered into a realm beyond normal human emotion. In the very moment when he should've looked angry, he looked tranquil. His eyes had a thick, religious glaze, and he appeared to me a man under some kind of spell. And though no sound was coming out, his lips were moving, whispering something too soft to make out. Laz stood up from the table and slowly started towards the exit. I got up too and followed him.

"Laz," I said. "What's the plan here?"

He said nothing, just kept walking. I sensed, then, that something terrible was about to happen.

"Laz!" I shouted and seized him by the arm, hoping to snap him out of his trance.

But Laz did not even look at me. With a strength that surprised me, he pried my hand off his arm and, still singing, marched out of the bar and towards Joe and the men.

Our presence startled Flag Boy and his crew. They stopped kicking Joe and looked at where we were standing, somewhat at me but mostly at Laz.

"What the hell are you supposed to be?" Flag Boy said and spit on the ground in Laz's general direction.

Laz did not respond. Instead, with great deliberation, he removed the black fedora from his head and placed it on the pavement. Then he removed his black shirt, folded it into a perfect square, and lay it beside the fedora. I struggled to process all that was happening. Joe was writhing down there on the pavement, bleeding from about five different places. The sky was still spitting gray sheets of rain. Flag Boy and his friends were alternating between talking shit to Joe and laughing at Laz. Then all of it, every component part of the crazy nightmare this day had become since we skipped our class to sit on the porch, was suddenly drowned out by what I saw on Laz's body, by what I saw on his skin.

I had never seen him with his shirt off and it was at that very moment that I realized why. Hundreds, and I mean hundreds, of scars covered his arms and his stomach and his chest. Some were flat and no bigger than a toothpick, but others were raised and closer in size to a pencil. I had never in my life seen anything like it. "Cutting" was not a word known or used at Clemson in the 1980's.

"You have one job, brother," Laz said to me, out of his spell and looking at Flag Boy with more rage than I had ever seen in a pair of human eyes.

"Anything," I said.

"Make sure you get Joe to Katie's."

I looked at Laz, and he nodded, and in that nod was more heart than the whole of Clemson combined. I knew there was no arguing with him. Had he asked me, I would've followed him into the fires of Hell.

"Can you do that?" Laz said.

"I can," I replied.

After that, Lazarus ran straight up to Flag Boy and drove his fist so hard into that man's face, that I could hear the crunch of nose bones from fifteen feet back. And if you think he stopped after that, you are wrong. With rain slamming down on everything, and blood leaking out of faces and mouths and hands, and me scooping Joe off the ground, and the whole world seeming at that moment to tremble and spin like a broken carousel, Laz kept punching and kicking and biting and screaming. For a moment, it did not matter that he was outnumbered. His fists were everywhere at once, dropping one after another of the men.

Remembering my promise, I dragged Joe to the moped and revved it. Joe croaked something then, but his mouth was full of blood and his voice too faded to hear. It could have been "Go." Or, it could have been "No." I never asked. I hit the gas and tore out of there, away from Old Son's and up towards that yellow house on the hill.

I allowed myself, just once, to look back. I have regretted this ever since. Because what I saw was that Flag Boy and his friends had regained the advantage. They were holding Laz down and beating him, mercilessly. Even still, that is not what I remember. What I remember is how Laz was smiling like a mad saint. How, even as they continued to punch him, he grinned directly into the center of their devilish faces and shouted something that sounded like, "Mine! Mine! Mine!"

I kept my word and got Joe to Katie's. After a little arguing and much weeping, she forgave him and, no shit, they have been blissed-out ever since. Meanwhile Laz's fate became a profound mystery that he himself would've delighted in. When he never showed up at Boudreaux, we went to Old

Son's and Sully told us Laz was taken by ambulance to the hospital in Oconee. We drove there but were turned away by a team of nurses nearly icy in their professionalism. Then, for weeks, nothing. Laz never came back to Boudreaux. Neither did he come back to Clemson. And wherever he ended up, he did not feel inclined to call or write. We tried several times to look him up, but no one even knew his last name.

In time, we all forgot him. Graduated, left, settled, and sunk. Clemson became a place you returned to for football. Our old house on Boudreaux was torn down to make room for a shopping center. But, for a while there, I looked forward to his return, waiting for the day we'd drag a box of beer out on the porch and start to roll back time and remember things. I'd sit in that room the color of regurgitated oatmeal and listen to our old watery-eyed prof carry on about the "Old South," and I'd think of the day I would tell Lazarus that he no longer fooled me. Because I had seen the light of his face in battle, and it was holy with truth and love, the face of a believer.

Dan Leach has published short stories, essays, and poems in *The New Orleans Review*, *Copper Nickel*, and *The Sun*. He has published two collections of short fiction: *Floods and Fires* (University of North Georgia, 2017) and *Dead Mediums* (Trident Press, 2022). A Greenville native, he currently lives in the lowcountry of South Carolina with his wife and four kids.